Long-Form Religious Porn

Fungasm Press

Portland + Los Angeles

PO Box 10065
Portland, OR 97296

ISBN: 978-1-62105-208-1

Copyright © 2015 by Laura Lee Bahr

Cover Art Copyright © 2015 by Jim Agpalza

Cover Design by Matthew Revert
www.matthewrevert.com

Edited by John Skipp

Printed in the USA.

Long-Form Religious Porn

Laura Lee Bahr

To the spirit of my teacher, Crerar Douglas, who helped my brain and heart blossom together toward the light.

"The greenhouse of personhood is a well-taught religion class."

Prologue:
The Love Story

She feels sick.

Yes, she might really throw up.

But that wouldn't look right. So instead she bites down on her tongue to continue writing the "f" in the blood of her former gay lover on the plaster-textured walls.

She has a moment where she can't quite remember how to spell it… N.O.S. F. E. R. T. U.? Yes? No? Does it matter? But then, of course, it matters if she wants it to look right — what kind of red herring would it be if she misspells the name of the dark lord she is supposedly serving?

And then she hears a gurgle-like moan, which she matches with her own moan of frustration and exhaustion.

He is *still* alive?

Really?

She had no idea how hard it actually is to bludgeon

someone to death with a decorative rock — even if they are chained up. She should probably use something else. A knife? A knife would do it. She could slit his throat and that would definitely end it, finally.

She opens the cabinet drawers on a search for something that would work. She finds a serrated bread knife, which she guesses will do the trick if she really puts her weight into it.

BUZZ.

Wait. Is that?

BUZZ. Held long like a desperate note.

It is the door of her apartment gate, outside. Someone is buzzing to come in. She walks over and presses 'TALK', leaving bits and pieces of whatever was on her hand on the call button.

"Hello?" she manages.

The voice through the static is shaking and holding back tears. The voice is the voice of the man whose relevance and existence will be debated in court: The Mystery Man. But he is no mystery to her.

There is a sigh like an answer to a prayer when he says her name, and a desperation she has never heard before from him, he whom she has only known as a desperate man.

"Dominique," he says. "Please, I need to come in."

She considers how to best phrase it. There is a simple way, if she can find it. She does.

"Now's not a good time," she says.

"I don't know what I'll do if I can't see you," he says. But he does know what he will do. And so does she. He will do what he's been considering doing since before she met him.

She doesn't want him to do that.

But then again, what could that possibly matter to her now?

But it does. It does matter.

The love story, if there is one, begins for her at this moment with this decision:

She holds down the button and lets him in.

PART ONE

Chapter 1:
A Sick Friend

" — and that is why it *must* be George Clooney."

Madeline Hunter is talking to be overheard, mouth full of guacamole. Her mother often told her talking with her mouth full was rude, but Madeline Hunter never shut up long enough to hear it. She swallows and drains her margarita, her eyes toward the door.

She continues talking in a litany that involves the following themes:

And why wouldn't he be in? The movie is POLITICAL. The movie is SEXUAL. The movie has MYSTERY and blood and gore. And it is extremely well written. And it isn't just Madeline that thinks so. The person who did coverage on it at ICM, he thought so, too; in fact, ICM (that's one of the twin towers of representation in Hollywood, folks) said they would come on and represent the script — but not with Madeline as a director. They would want to attach a *name* director.

Madeline practically spits the last sentence, and then waves a hand through her black bob and strikes a pose like she is all Louise Brooks in "Pandora's Box."

"Fuck them! It is so fucking hard for women directors in this town. This town is filled with misogynists. That's what drove someone like Dominique Colt to commit bloody murder the way she did. Don't any of them get that? Right?"

Dieter Künstwerk, her companion across the booth, is not his usual responsive self. Normally, he'd already have fired back twelve witty rejoinders and a partridge in a pear tree. But he barely manages a head nod, after a pause so pregnant she is about to induce it with another "*right?*" She notices for the first time that Dieter is not his usual dapper self, either. He looks like shit, frankly.

They are meeting at Casa Vega, where George Clooney is rumored to show up from time to time, which is as dark as a tomb even in the daytime.

Dieter has his sunglasses on. And he is not eating anything, meaning Madeline is eating the guacamole, the chips and salsa, and was the only one who ordered a margarita and a veggie burrito. She certainly doesn't need to eat all this food by herself, even if she is only behind the camera.

"Hey, you feeling okay, Deets?"

Dieter shakes his head. He had some eye surgery thing done — that's why the sunglasses — and he has been having other medical issues lately.

Madeline gets a twinge of worry. Here she has been prattling on about George Clooney and Dieter might be dying. Fuck. What kind of friend is she, anyway? A shitty one, she knows it, but Dieter's the best friend she's got. She hopes to fuck he's okay. Who else will listen to her bullshit?

"So what's the diagnosis? What do you got? Is it some weird illness or something?"

Dieter shakes his head. "No, it's not an illness *per se*," he says with a bit of a theatrical flip of his wrist. "It's a condition."

"Well, what kind of condition?"

"It's a sensitivity to sunlight."

"Jesus, you are in the wrong town for that," Madeline says. "All we got is sunlight."

Dieter manages a weak smile. He has started to notice that.

She asks if doctors are making progress. How does this condition improve? Dieter says it is a chronic condition. In fact it is only going to get worse.

"Shit! No more beach days?" Madeline says.

And Dieter starts to cry.

Madeline is appalled at her own insensitivity. Why, George Clooney could walk in at any moment and see her with this friend who clearly looks like he has something fatal and she is making him cry and she would look even worse when she left her sick crying friend and approached Clooney to hand him a script. But Dieter would understand. He is as shallow and opportunist as anyone. He would leave her drunk and puking at a bar to go home with a random hot bear in leather any day of the week… and had.

Madeline moves over to sit next to Dieter. Who cares if now she no longer has a view of the door. Fuck George Clooney. In one hundred years they would all be dead and who would care anyway whether she made this movie or if she ever met George Clooney or directed his next big thing. She is smart enough to be philosophical about everything, when it comes right down to it. Her heart: Ice cold.

Speaking of which, that is Dieter to the touch. She puts her arm around him and is even more alarmed. He is really thin and pasty. She holds his little shoulders as they rock.

"Hey, hey!" she says. "It'll be all right. I think. Won't it?"

Dieter shakes his head.

So he is dying then, that is it. Shit! She should write a movie about this. This would be a totally guerilla style indie. Fuck Hollywood. She doesn't need their shit. She'll just get a camera and chronicle the death of Dieter.

The Death of Dieter: It would be so moving, so sad, the story of a twenty-eight year old destined to die of some strange disease.... and, of course, the story of their eight year friendship, begun as sophomores at University of Southern California (USC), when she convinced him to skip class and go watch the Dominique Colt court case instead —

"I wanna stop, Mads."

Now that is interesting. Stop? She adjusts her thinking. Okay, so he's lied to her. He is on drugs. Shit! Another stupid friend on drugs. She has no time in her life for stupid fucking addicts. Goddamn it Dieter, what a shit-head!

"How can I help?" Madeline asks, in her most helpful voice, realizing immediately how much she has no desire to help.

Dieter takes off his sunglasses.

Madeline almost screams and jumps out of the booth. His eyes are fucking RED. Not red like he's been crying. Red like his pupils are totally Amityville Horror Pig "GET OUT" fucking Red.

"Can you keep a secret?" he asks.

She could not, never had, but she nods.

Chapter 2:
Mads and Deets,
Deets and Mads

Madeline, in her dinged green Nissan Versa, follows Dieter's gray Scion on the 101 South. She plays a montage of their eight-year friendship as she drives, Arcade Fire albums providing the soundtrack:

— it starts with the opening choral voices of "Wake Up"

— a quick shot of her and Dieter in their film production class

— jump cut to him holding the boom for a scene they were shooting in which these two horrible actors are trying to look natural eating burgers and Dieter softly singing with a creepy German expressionism, "You are being followed by a Boom… Shadow," in an atonal interpretation of Cat Stevens' "Moonshadow"

— reaction shot of the rabbit-faced actress who doesn't get it, but Deets and Mads are sharing a look

— now it's "The Sprawl," and they are walking across campus, almost holding hands and laughing their asses off

— end Montage.

Madeline liked dudes and stuff, but Dieter was not the type of dude she would like. Dieter liked dudes, too, but not the dudes that Madeline liked, so they got on like a super-virus. More montage:

The two of them seeing bands together, talking shit, talking movies, drinking Absinthe, skipping their film history class to go and watch the Dominique Colt case on TV in her dorm room. After graduating, both of them trying to get real film crew experience, eating Subway five-dollar foot-longs and drinking all the free coffee they could from Dieter's job at Starbucks. Dieter getting a job at Flashy Talent Agency, the parties they would go to, drinking all they could at open bars, the youtube music videos they'd make of Dieter's favorite bands. Dieter's soap opera relationships with bear men, from B-movie producers to bar-owners. But really, theirs is the only relationship they could both count on for symbiotic fulfillment. Them on the couch in his apartment, her feet in his lap as they are watching obscure independent movies, their eyes meeting in a mutual understanding as they snarf/laugh at the same weird thing.

Mads and Deets, Deets and Mads.

In memoriam of Dieter Künstwerk, my best friend who died young, she thinks, tears welling up in her eyes as she searches for a parking place.

Dieter lives in a sad sardine can of a building with bars on the windows off of Franklin and First Street in Hollywood.

Dieter parked in his covered parking, while Madeline circles for ten minutes trying to find a spot.

He's been texting her constantly since he'd parked.

-Waiting for you-

She texts back as she drives.

-Looking for parking-

-Try on third-

-Nothing-

A person is honking at her for driving slow, and passing her on the left. She casually gives him the finger.

She ranks and categorizes her friends and realizes with a wave of guilt and regret that Dieter has been her closest friend since college. She's lost touch with most of her girlfriends, who were now mostly into their relationships with their boyfriends, and she alone has remained single, hyper-focused on moving forward from short films to make a break-out feature. She had a series of "awards" like any indie moviemaker, for her short film, "Swallow," the story of a woman who becomes a bird…

…Finally!

-Found a spot on fifth-

-Fucking street parking-

She locks her car and walks the trash-lined streets of Hollywood to Dieter's apartment. Dieter stands outside his building like a bad omen, a black umbrella in hand.

"Hey," Madeline says.

Dieter responds by opening his front door, bars and all, to her. "After you," he says in a low voice.

Dieter closes the huge umbrella he had been using to walk the twelve feet from his car to his door, and, with a couple of head turns to make sure he isn't seen, he shuts the door behind Madeline.

The wall-to-wall dream-deferred-forever carpet and half-broken vertical blinds are made all the more depressing — and alarming — by black foil on the windows. The usual scent of the apartment – that of man/boy and European cologne with the finish of leftover food that her nose had always identified as "Dieter's" – now has a metallic and damp bouquet that makes the margarita and enchilada in her belly do a nasty dance.

How long has it been since she visited Dieter? She has been busy being dicked around by Hollywood phonies, sure, and that has taken a lot of time and energy, but has it really been so long?

Madeline has never been known to quell or quake or quiver, but she is doing all three as the door shuts softly.

He lights a candle.

Madeline expects him to pull out a spoon and start cooking something on it, but instead he takes his sunglasses off. In the candlelight, his eyes glow with a ruby-like intensity that would have been beautiful if it weren't so fucking creepy.

"What I am about to reveal to you," he says, "you must never reveal to anyone, even upon the pain of death."

"Oh, well, that's okay. You don't need to tell me — " Madeline starts, but Dieter has not waited for her response so he's uttered the unutterable before she can stop him and she talks over his big reveal:

"Madeline, I am becoming a Vampire."

There is a moment of silence.

"Huh," she says. "Now why would you go and do something like that?"

"I was just looking into them online, and then I met with them, and now I'm already a Level 3."

"Level 3?"

14

Madeline knows a thing or two about The Vampires:

As it is a newish cult, there is still plausible deniability of the obvious aging of its members (and leader) and the deaths of a few (whom they claimed had 'killed themselves' by ceasing to drink blood.) There is, like all newly formed cults (and most certainly expected in a fucking Vampire cult) violence and threats against members leaving and revealing its secrets.

But every fucking Vampire is so fucking excited to be a fucking Vampire they can hardly keep it to themfuckingselves and have to fucking share, usually with a retarded statement like, "What I am about to reveal to you must be protected with your life, or it will cost you your life."

The Church of the Immortal Order, or The Order, as they preferred to be called, had, as of late, been undergoing a major Hollywood PR push, recruiting name actors and publicizing with billboards on Sunset that say, "LEARN the TRUTH! You CAN live forever!" with a handsome man and woman with a knowing smile (showing no teeth) on it and the "The Church of the Immortal Order: A church for the rare individual." There had been some bad press a few years back with the Dominique Colt case, who claimed she had been involved with them — which they had vehemently denied, and threatened to sue her for libel (which, in addition to her capital charges of murder, seemed laughable).

"Didn't you say you wanted to stop?" Madeline says, glad she was listening for once in her life.

Dieter nods, and his red eyes well up with tears.

"Well, let's talk about how to stop," Madeline says, remembering how her nice therapists have talked to her in the past when she has been in and out of therapy for various causes.

"That's what I'm trying to tell you — I'm a Level 3! I can't just '*stop*!'"

And then Dieter goes on to tell her how there are all these levels and processes and sacred rituals. Level 1, you don't even do any transformation, you just volunteer, find out more, become part of the community, are considered an acolyte. Some people live at Level 1 for decades, even centuries (Madeline does not point out that they have not been around for centuries, but listens and nods). Level 2 involves actual initiation and the "drinking of blood." Level 3 is the beginnings of "transformation."

So they don't age, they begin a series of injections — Botox, as far as Madeline can piece together, as well as HGH to help them build muscle tissue. He is calling it something else, but Madeline is trying to separate their bullshit terminology from the actual stuff movie stars have been doing since they could. They also begin bleaching their skin.

And whereas at Level 2 they eat rare meat, at Level 3 they begin the process of "undoing mortal consumption" by what sounds to Mads like a glorified anorexia with glucose injections and drinking "blood" (which is not human blood, Dieter assures her, not yet, but a protein based red substance that has been created for modern Vampires; human blood, like most human food, is toxic).

So, for the past six months, while Madeline has been absorbed in trying to get a script to Clooney and raising money for the Dominique Colt picture, Dieter has been not eating, bleaching his skin, and getting Botox even though he is only twenty-eight.

Dieter's eyes, of course, aren't actually red. He is wearing red contacts. And he has eye dilators to help him see at night. He doesn't say what he and his new Vampire friends are doing at night. Whatever it is, his allusions to it sound sketchy as fuck.

"All right, Madeline," he says. (Why is he calling her Madeline, he always calls her 'Mads'?) "My confession is over. Do you have any questions?"

Well, there are a million of them, beginning with, *are you fucking stupid or what?* But she decides to take a different tack.

"So... when you see a cross, do you, like... freak out?"

Dieter starts talking, and it sounds like a script. Like he is a movie actor playing the role of Dieter, a poor suck brainwashed by a wacko cult.

"The Cross, of course, is meaningless in itself, but in terms of its semiotic value, there is a despicable history. The Cross represents an archaic tribal god, a lack of responsibility and control over one's destiny which one places outside oneself. It is a paradigm in which the reasonless act of exchanging fluids from impure orifices and shoving body parts into another creates life and therefore death.

"But the first rule of The Order is to spit that truth back out. Vampires do not die. They do not copulate. They create each other by the same manner in which they feed themselves — creation is a conscious act. They can either consume you, or, allow you to, like them, become immortal. This is why Vampires cannot tolerate the Cross. They find the very symbol viscerally offensive. To celebrate the bloody sacrificial death of God's own supposed Son — a meaningless, criminal's death — and to celebrate that as salvation. It goes against a Vampire's very nature. Also, the Cross has been used for centuries as a symbol of hate against Vampires. Like many symbols throughout the ages, the power of the symbol takes on greater meaning or hate depending on who is using it. Vampires are natural enemies of the weak, the pathetic, and the ignorant. The Cross is the symbol of these people. "

Monologue finished, Madeline knows she should respond. She says the only thing in her head.

"Whoa," she says.

Dieter stares her.

"Garlic?" she asks.

Dieter narrows his red eyes at her. "Really Madeline, I thought you'd be more sophisticated than to ask questions like this."

"I'm just trying to understand, that's all, Deets. And why do you keep calling me 'Madeline'?"

Mads and Deets, their pet names. Deets and Mads. Their band name. Mads and Deets — her gay not-husband. It's her fault. She has been too self-obsessed. She thinks of when he called her three months ago, and how she had just found out she had a connection to George Clooney's assistant. Then, if she had called him back, met him for drinks like he'd wanted, maybe he wouldn't have gotten so mixed up in this shit.

"What do they think of all this at your job?" she asks.

"They love it," he says. "The Vampires are blowing up in Hollywood."

"Really?" How could Madeline, a self-respecting wanna-be director, be so out of the loop?

Dieter flashes her a filed canine. "They could help you a lot, Madeline. A lot. You'd be surprised who's a Vampire in this town."

"Is George Clooney a Vampire?"

Dieter closes his mouth. "Not yet. But…," he says. "Vince Vaughn is."

"Vince Vaughn? But he doesn't have red eyes or anything."

Vince, according to Dieter, is in the C class — they have

a different track. Celebrities. Because of his connections at Flashy Talent Agency, Dieter is in with this track. He might even be able to connect her to the… Vince… Vaughn.

Madeline thinks about Vince Vaughn in her movie. She doesn't like it.

"What's the point of being a Vampire if you don't look like one?" This is all very confusing to Madeline — it would make sense if it's just about look or mystique. Maybe Vince Vaughn just busts out his red eyes for parties?

"You are missing the point," Dieter huffs. "We are all preparing. These are levels of preparations as we wait for the return of our Master."

"Dracula?"

Dieter does not look happy with this response. "No, Madeline. Really, don't be stupid. He is no one you have heard of in fairy tales, but I would love to tell you about him, the Master…"

Basically, they are waiting. Waiting for some dude who lived for thousands of years but looks twenty who left to roam the earth and sky to find loyal followers. When the Master comes, they will have their final transformation. Until then, they need to gradually undergo this transitory, gentle phase from human to Vampire. And wait for the Master to come and stick his beloved fangs into their jugulars and suck them into immortality.

As he speaks, he has a sense of glazed rapture in his voice, so Madeline reminds him again:

"You want out, though, right?"

"I can't, though," he says, dreamily. "I'm already a Level 3. I already know too much. They'll never let me go. And…," he looks directly at Madeline. "I'm not sure I have the strength to leave them."

Mads nods as solemnly as she can, trying to think of a game plan. "Well, Dieter, I am glad that you have found a group of people you really respond to," she says, in her best 'I'm-an-adult-and-I-speak-like-one' voice.

Dieter hisses (really, that's not a figure of a speech).

"Um," says Mads. "Did that offend you?"

"It's not about that! It's not fucking about that!" He has little spittle flying and Mads realizes if she hadn't had a proper meal in a week she might be a spitting hissing thing, too. She once experimented with anorexia but it was only a day before she was too weak to go on. And bulimia for almost a week until her uvula hurt. She has accepted that being thought of as poor-willed and muffin-topped would be her cross to bear. Cross! Fuck! Why did she think 'Cross'? Could he read thoughts?

"So what's it about?" she asks, trying not to think of anything but looking as understanding and supportive as possible.

Dieter looks at her with an expression that makes Mads want to peel herself out of her skin.

"It's about living forever, Madeline."

Madeline's phone buzzes: Justin Timberlake's "I'm Bringing Sexy Back." She never thought she would love that ring-tone so much.

"It's Julian, I have to answer that," Madeline says. Her purse is around her arm. The light of her phone is showing the frozen face of Julian Montegreen, a batshit crazy agent she hit it off with at a party. He also knows Dieter.

"Hi Julian," Madeline says in her most casual voice.

"What's happening hot stuff?" asks Julian.

"Oh nothing, just hanging out with Deets," she says.

"Does he know?" she mouths to Dieter, and then doing fangs with her two front fingers. Dieter shakes his head and gives her an alarmed expression.

"Can I fondle what's hanging out?" Julian asks.

"Uh...," she mutters. Julian, for some reason that truly escapes Madeline, has this act that he desperately wants to sleep with her. Maybe it's his operating system. "Sure," she finishes. He never will fondle anything on her and they both know it.

"Did the Persian connection come through?" he asks. Two weeks ago, the owner of the largest import store in Glendale had sounded interested in putting up 40K for the picture, but he has since said he's decided to redo his front lawn instead.

"Negative," says Madeline.

"Okay, well then, fuck Persia," Julian says. "I got something better. I was mentioning the project to Pussy Foot, and I sent her a script and she's in love with it."

"Pussy Foot?"

"She's a big burlesque act in Long Beach, and she's got a huge fetish clientele."

"What kind of fetish?"

"Madeline. Come on."

She's got a lot on her mind... she can't quite...

"It's her last name."

Foot. Yes. Right. Foot fetish. "I know, got it. So what?"

Madeline is now fully engrossed with Julian, and notices Dieter's pacing the way she'd notice the buzzing of a gnat.

"She also does some BDSM stuff, and that's what really got her about the Colt story. She wants to play Dominique Colt."

"Well, anyone would want to play Dominique Colt, the way I've written her."

"And she's willing to invest 50,000 to do it."

Mads sighs deeply. 50,000 is something, sure. It's not the two million dollar budget she was hoping for, but as a first time director, for her first feature, without a star… maybe she shouldn't look a gift foot in the mouth.

"Let's set up a meeting," she says.

She hears a door shut. Dieter is shutting his bedroom door.

Madeline takes the opportunity to turn on lights. But when she flips on the one in the living room, she is greeted by a weak lamp in the corner. The overheads in the kitchen area are out completely. Ditto the living room overhead.

Still, she can see some more of the room.

Madeline is spooked by how clean it is.

Big bound volumes on his coffee table. And stacks and stacks of headshots. One stack has large Xs across the faces.

Julian suggests they meet tonight. Madeline's schedule is open since REAL REELS hasn't had any shows for her to close-caption lately, but she hems and haws like she has to really figure out how to clear her calendar.

Madeline suggests Casa Vega.

Julian says elsewhere, Casa Vega is too crowded at night.

Madeline insists on the place, but will change the date. She does her "I'm so busy" litany "but looking for an opening" speech and says she can make it during Happy Hour tomorrow.

Julian says it sounds good and he'll check with the Foot.

"Wanna lick ya," he says in his characteristic parting phraseology.

"Yeah, later," she says in hers.

Dieter opens his bedroom door as Mads presses the red "end call" button.

"What's with the creepy X headshots?" she asks.

Dieter doesn't answer the question. "The Order could help you, Madeline. Do you know how far I've moved up the ladder at my job since I joined them?"

"Level 3?" Madeline ventures.

"Ha ha," he says.

"Why do I need Vampires when I've got Julian? He just got me a lead to some money if I attach a certain person. Ugh. Let me see who this person is."

She starts to look up Pussy Foot on her phone.

"Don't tell Julian," Dieter warns.

"Or you'll have to kill him?" Mads ventures.

"Just don't say anything. You said you'd keep it a secret. You don't fuck with The Order, Madeline."

"Or you end up a headshot with an X through it?"

Dieter suddenly throws over the coffee table, the headshots falling to the ground with some flutter, the bound volumes like stones.

"Well," says Madeline, after a moment.

Dieter has never done anything like that before, either. Whole new Dieter. Not a Dieter she likes. "I guess I should be going."

"Please don't," he says, so softly and desperately that if she had a heart it would break a little. "Please."

"You said you wanted help, Dieter, that's all. But it doesn't sound like that is actually what you want."

"What I actually want is you, Madeline."

And he bends so close to her she can smell his breath — an Atkins diet sort of smell- — and then swear to God he starts to move his mouth toward her neck.

Mads forgets that she knows Dieter is a fuck-up pansy, a German joiner anxious to forget his Nazi-guilt piss-poor heritage. She forgets she knows what he looks like when he is crying over a boy, or how lame he dances. An instinct kicks in and she kicks back. She knees Dieter — her like, best boy-girlfriend like, ever — so hard in his poor nuts.

And then before she can remember to apologize or ask if he's okay, she is running/falling out of the chair she was sitting in, and is racing toward the front door of his apartment.

The door is locked, of course, but she turns the locks with an ease she never has had any of the countless times she spent here, as if her hands had been training all this time for this moment. Lock after lock unlocks, and she throws the front door open to a rectangle of bright and angry sunlight.

She plunges into it like a mermaid into water.

And swims for her life into that sun.

Chapter 3:
The Foot

Her given name was Patricia Frank, but doesn't that just suit her like "lipstick on a pig?" She drawls out all the words and every word sounds like warm honey moving slow on her tongue all the way from North Carolina.

She has skin the color of toffee and eyes that are an impossible shade of gold and are most likely, Mads thinks, contacts. The feet are kept in soft taupe shoes — never heels, for "mobility in my feet is essential for my line of work," she explains.

Madeline is a bit jittery, a bit on edge, not that Julian or Ms. Foot seem to notice.

"I watched that speech Dominique Colt gave at the end of her trial about a hundred times. It just made me cry it was so sad. Woman pleading for her life about to be crucified by the system." Pussy's eyes are liquid compassion. "I knew then that this was a character I understood."

Madeline has to be honest that Pussy is a far 'outside the box' choice. She is older, she is darker, she has an accent.

Pussy can lose the accent, Pussy can be ageless, Pussy can do anything, "but turn myself white. But I think having a woman of color play Dominique makes the character that much more faceted, don't you think?"

Madeline half nods, shrugs. "You can really lose the accent?"

"I am first and foremost an actress," she says in a flawless cracker-white-lady imitation. She massages her left foot with a casual air like it indicates nothing but subliminal relief. "But a girl always has to make a living."

Julian laughs like it is a joke. Julian has the unfortunate habit of laughing constantly at things that aren't funny or meant to be funny, like it's his way of filling a pause. That, paired with being 5'2 and looking like the love child of Joe Pesci and Ron Weasley, makes his consistent hypersexual comments an obvious shtick.

"It's the world's oldest profession!" he chimes in agreeably. He is usually much dirtier, but he is on his best behavior for the Foot.

"Why do you keep looking toward the bar?" Pussy asks Madeline. "I'm not used to people looking past me for someone better over my shoulder."

Julian chokes a little on a chip, mortified that Madeline might have offended her. But Madeline merely shrugs and finishes what she is drinking. She slept a fitful four hours last night, with crazy dreams about Dieter floating outside her window. She's been scared shitless. Pleasing Pussy's ego at this point seems a low priority on her list, 50K or not.

"She's looking for George Clooney," Julian says, with a barking laugh.

"George Clooney?"

"It's rumored that he comes here sometimes," Julian continues with hyena-like delivery, "and Madeline is a little stalker-like in her obsession."

"Oh, well, then *that* is understandable," Pussy says with a throaty laugh. "I'd love to put a Foot on that man."

"I want him to play the Mystery Man," Madeline says, all business.

"Oooh, yeah!" says Pussy. "Wouldn't he just steam that role right up? But isn't he a little…I don't know… *too* good looking?"

Madeline darts her eyes to Pussy's with a challenging stare. "Not anymore. He's *old,* now."

"Oh, right," says Pussy, thoughtfully.

Madeline moves then, very suddenly, in a weird duck.

"What?" asks Julian.

"It's *Mr. Snow,*" Madeline whispers, head down.

"Who?" Julian asks, looking exactly where Madeline didn't want him to.

"Switch places with me."

"Why?" asks Julian.

"I see my math teacher from high school at the bar."

"So?"

"So, I don't want him to see me!"

"Why?"

"Because then he might come and talk to me!"

"So?"

Madeline glares at him. "Is there anything more awkward than seeing your former math teacher in a bar in the middle of the day? And Christ, he looks like shit. Just switch places with me."

Julian complies and Madeline ducks under the table and

comes up the other side. Julian, for his part, moves with a semi-apologetic air to Pussy, but then again, he's batshit crazy and Pussy gives people foot jobs for a living, so no one's really judging anyone.

When Madeline safely has her back to Mr. Snow, she continues, but in a softer voice. "But keep an eye out for Clooney," she tells Julian.

He gives her a half-salute.

"What would you do if you saw him?" Pussy asks.

"George Clooney? I'd give him a script, of course."

"Isn't that very…," Pussy thinks for the word and settles on "…green?"

"Yes, it's super green, but this is what I have been debased to, Ms. Foot. Let me explain."

And Madeline explains:

Madeline understands that George Clooney is busy, and that he is a little old for the role of the Mystery Man, but it is just the type of deep, socio-politically affective role he gravitates toward. If he just saw the script, if he just read the first page for Christ's sake, he'd be in. She thinks she has a solid lead. For one thing, she knows an acquaintance of his assistant. So in addition to the casting director who she already paid $3000 to be on-board (to just say they could not get George Clooney's manager to return their calls — hell, Madeline herself could have got George Clooney to not return her calls, she didn't need to pay someone $3000 for that), she also knows Jennifer Klienzemen, who knows George Clooney's assistant. George Clooney is notoriously nice to his assistant. If he bought his assistant a house, why wouldn't he at least take the trouble, when she was assisting him in all aspects of his life, to read a script?

"So," Madeline finishes, "I am not going to just say, 'George Clooney, here is a script,' I am going to play the moment with the details I know about his assistant, and then maybe fake a heart attack or something. Or maybe I'll do something completely different. Whatever it is, put him in the same room with me and it's a done deal. I got something."

Pussy breaks into a grin. "I like you," she says. She places one eyelid down in the sultriest wink Mads has ever seen. "You're a hustler."

"'Gimme that funk, that sweet, that nasty, that gushi stuff- but don't bullshit me.'" Mads drops some Jay-Z without missing a beat.

That seals it.

"I got 50K for this project with me attached as Dominique," Pussy says.

"Interesting," Madeline says. "But that's less than a tenth of what I'm aiming for, which is already very small for a project of this scope. That amount will just cover the day we shoot the death scene. I mean, killing people like that — she pretty much did that for the price of a rock, stockings, a couple of chains and a knife. But to make it *look* like that happened — that's money. With you attached I lose negotiating for a star with a bigger name who could guarantee more of a return in the box office. "

Pussy blinks.

It's a dangerous wager and Mads knows it. Right now, this is the first offer she's had that is any sort of money. Julian's eyes are wide, and he has forgotten to laugh.

Dominique gives a Mona Lisa of a smile. "I bring the first 50K and will find us 150 more. I'm attached to play Dominique via contract, which also guarantees you as the director. No one can negotiate *you* out for a bigger name."

Touché.

Madeline shrugs. "We can start the ball rolling with that."

Julian hoots like a stripper just took off her top and raises his martini glass.

"With your brains and my feet, who knows what kind of trouble we'll get into," Pussy says, raising her glass of sparkling Perrier.

"All right then," Madeline says, raising her margarita. "To a new vision of Dominique Colt."

They all drink.

Pussy smacks her lips.

"We'll need some re-writes, of course," Foot purrs.

"Hmmmm???" says Madeline, like she misheard.

"Well, as we discussed already, I obviously don't look a thing like a fish-stick white girl like the real Dominique Colt." And she laughs, showing a perfect little gap in her two front teeth like Alfred E Neuman.

"Oh, yeah, there are lines about her looks I'll tweak," Madeline says, taking the last of the chips and signaling for another basket.

Pussy looks thoughtful. "And I want her to seem more smart."

Madeline chokes on the chip she was still eating. "Smart?"

"Yeah, you're obviously a smart girl. Let's give her some smart lines. Have her quote philosophy and talk about... oh, philosophers."

Madeline will not deign to chew at this point. She lets the saliva-sogged chip stay in her mouth like the Wafer Host, reminding her that one should never chew their Lord. Not that she'd ever been Catholic or anything.

Julian is nodding. "Madeline is hot for smart, smart lines, smart dialogue, she can smart it up no problem."

And Pussy starts riffing with him like they are writing this picture, like it is their fucking baby, like they have any fucking clue about anything:

"Maybe she's still in school…like *graduate* school or something! She's on her way to be somebody and do something great with her life, but she just gets all mixed up because she doesn't really know anything *but* book smarts…"

Madeline isn't sure what to say. What to do. How to proceed. Pussy Foot, some C list BDSM internet personality — who should be down on all fours and giving her free foot jobs or whatever the fuck she does — is asking her for *re-writes* of her brilliant script?

Pussy keeps going and has been going on for some time while Madeline's face is blank — blank as someone trying not to breathe because she might hurl if she does.

" — and so when Dominique's mind snaps — " Pussy snaps and stares straight at Mads like a hypnotist. "Awake!"

But Madeline is in a nightmare. "Re-writes?" is all she can manage.

Foot's face gives a look of concern. "That seems standard for a star, right? To get some re-writes?' Her lilting Carolina dialect now sounds like the sinister song of torture.

Madeline still can't respond.

It is the best lead she has had since ICM passed on her. It's the only offer of actual money that has been on the table. And it is just some simple re-writes to make it suit her star. And make her star seem smart.

What's the big deal?

She swallows.

Julian kicks her under the table. Hard.

She nods. "Of course." And then she nods harder and gives a 'pshaw hand. "Of *course.*"

And they all laugh, like at the end of a sitcom.

Meanwhile, at the bar, Mr. Snow glances over, hearing the saddest sound in the world: People fake laughing at something fake funny. He thinks he sees one of his students from years ago. He hopes she doesn't see him. But then, what does it matter now that all that water has gone over all those burned bridges.

But still.

He pays his tab quickly and slinks out.

Chapter 4:
Bertie Snow in
the Winters of His
Discontent

Ten years prior, in the perpetual summer that is Los Angeles, even in December, Bertie Snow played Santa Claus for his wife and 8-year-old son, Parker.

As he sweat beneath the made-in-some-factory-by-enslaved-elves scratchy white beard and red suit and did his best "Ho! Ho! Ho!" he saw not magic or Christmas spirit in his child's eyes, but contempt.

Clearly, if this were Santa Claus, it was a real letdown.

But that didn't surprise him, nor that he had gone through the trouble of dressing like Santa at all. Had his son ever believed in Santa? Wasn't his son just humoring them by even pretending to believe? Nor was the distracted look on his wife's face unexpected, as she half-smiled through his jolly delivery of the "naughty" and "nice" things Parker had done. That stressed, over-worked, under-appreciated half-near tears cloud had hung about her head threatening to burst for years, now.

What surprised him was that he had no emotion, no disappointment, no sense of anything about the realization that neither his son nor his wife were interested in the grand dance he was now delivering.

Wherefore this pantomime?

He cut it short. "I must return back to my sleigh!" he said, and proceeded to "ho-ho-ho!" his way out the front door before sneaking into the garage. He pulled off the beard and the suit, getting down to his undershirt and boxers and then realized it wasn't just his wife and kid.

How long had it been since *he* had given a shit? About anything?

Oh, he'd put up a valiant effort. Yes, he was a man who wore full three-piece suits to teach high school when the other teachers at the Well-Spring School wore t-shirts and sandals.

Mr. Snow, at the time, had lived through the earth doing 45 full sun rotations. He was set as a personality, and set in an occupation. He had distinguished himself in the causal, "whole-student" environment by his insistence on formality with a wink, whenever possible. He was also a dynamic and rigorous mathematics instructor, who made jokes that were slightly off-color but invisible to those without a sophisticated sense of humor. He was well-liked by his students, his colleagues and the administrators. The suit, if not the daily persistence, indicated involvement in his own life — giving a shit.

And then he was a very involved husband and father. He

had a brilliant son who already understood negative exponents and wanted to be a software engineer. His wife, Joanne, was a kind and lovely woman who taught kindergarten, who took delight in the simple things, who had filled his life with joy and finger-paint.

But he felt no joy in it anymore.

He was moving from point A to B and back to A, only to go back to B and back to A again over the course of so many days, just completing the task in front of him:

Wake up, shower, shave, put on his three-piece suit, drive to work, get out of the car, walk up the steps to his classroom, take attendance, try and teach children, grade papers, go home, have a drink, help make dinner, eat dinner, drink again, watch TV, fall asleep and then again and again and again so many times he had forgot if he was anything else but this routine.

And then one morning he woke up, with his alarm, six a.m., and a thought, much stronger than even his alarm, said very clearly, distinctly:

"*It's time to kill yourself, Bert.*"

He had never been the suicidal type, never even considered it in his bleakest of days, so the thought was so startling — so utterly new, so utterly -

"*Kill yourself.*"

Whose voice was that?

And that is when he looked around at his insides, and noticed that everything was heavy and sticky in him, like oatmeal left for days, and where his heart once was was just gray gravy and —

"*It will help. It will help.*"

The thing that was surprising, as he showered, as he shaved, was that as he considered the possibility, it actually cheered him up.

Suddenly he looked into his bright blue eyes with the look of a predator, sizing up his prey. *This man,* he thought, *what a pathetic excuse for a man. This man clearly deserves to die. What use is he?*

He mused more on this as he put on the three-piece suit, which now seemed like the stupidest costume of all — because he had worn this suit because he had given a shit, because he had wanted to stand out and show them that he respected them and respected his work. And now…

He drank his coffee and smiled at his wife who was rushing about, getting ready for her day at work. When he looked at his son playing games on his phone at the kitchen table he thought about his life-insurance policy. He thought about the nice life his wife and kid could have without him. They would have tragedy to bind them together. Tragedy.

And their lives would be forever marked and held together by their shared depth of understanding of this, his death, which they would not know was suicide but would think was an accident. Maybe they could even sue some corporation, too, and get more money. Oh, this made him happy. How could he best kill himself and incriminate some evil corporation?

And for the first day in as long as he could remember, he found himself humming.

"Aren't you cheerful," Joanne said. It wasn't a compliment. He could tell she was jealous, bitter. Why, Joanne was probably just as depressed as he was! Why hadn't he seen it before?

He kissed her on the cheek.

"Why not be cheerful?" he said. "We have a great life."

His son looked at him like he was tripping. Even at age 8, the kid knew bullshit.

"We do," Bert insisted. "We are all healthy, we can afford

food, health insurance, and some luxury items, we have a great kid, and we both have jobs. We are not discriminated against, hated, or in a war-torn country. We are not descendents of genocide. We are not persecuted for our beliefs. We are educated. We don't have student loans. Our kid is not retarded. What do we have to complain about?"

Joanne narrowed her eyes at him.

"You're not funny," she said.

Chapter 5:
Positive Thinking

And it was thus that Bert got his spring back in his step, even in the abnormal winter storms that year in Los Angeles that poured rain down upon its woefully unprepared citizens. Houses fell off hills in the canyons with mudslides. Black mold seeped into walls where it would grow and infect inhabitants for years to come. Drivers drove straight into each other like water wasn't wet.

But Bert felt better.

Because of this thought: *Well, soon I will kill myself and it will all be over.*

Or when a student or parent or administrator required his attention, to throttle it with doldrum details of insignificance, the thought was there, too:

Well, soon I will be dead — won't that be a surprise!

This new thought of happiness kept him going for two

solid weeks. Then it sort of sank into the background, like his pipe dream to become a stand-up comedian. And the depression started to swaddle around him again, embracing him in its tepid, oatmeal arms. He started to forget about killing himself, what with his kid's upcoming birthday party, with the crazy new curriculum requirements, with…

Chapter 6:
A Year Has Passed

Shit.

It was Christmas again.

You aren't going to do it.

Of course he wasn't. He hadn't even thought about *how* to do it, just that he *should* do it, meaning of course, he wasn't going to do it at all.

But he must! Why, thinking about killing himself was the only thing keeping him going! He had to plan!

Why, of course, he had neglected the most important part — the steps needed to actually do it! He scolded himself. "Silly Bertie, you are like a student forgetting to show their steps and not knowing what to do when they get lost in finding the roots of the quadratic. Back to the beginning."

He must kill himself. That was what was required. It had to look like an accident for insurance money. Although he wasn't sure if that was just an urban legend or if the policy actually prohibited getting money from suicide. He'd need to investigate his policy, which would mean finding where it was stored. Or calling the agency — no, he couldn't do that. Either way, money or not, he didn't want to traumatize his poor wife and kid with his truth that his life was suffocating him. It wasn't their fault. He was the one who had asked to marry Joanne. He was the one who impregnated her. He was the one who said at a lovely Unitarian service that they would support and love each other until the end of their lives. So, well, he just had to bring his in a little sooner.

He looked around at the people who had died in his life. Most had been done in by some sort of cancer, or a car accident. Could he trust himself to initiate a car accident? What if that just left him paralyzed, or worse, what if he killed someone else *and* paralyzed himself? That would not do.

Could he contract cancer?

He could take up smoking, but that would take some time, more time than he was willing to give it.

No... no... no...

He thought of all sorts of 'accidents' that could befall him. Being hit by a car or, even better, a bus? Again, there was the distinct possibility he wouldn't die but suffer even more greatly through a long, paralyzed crippled life. Shattering his head by falling down the stairs? Falling off a tall building?

No, no, all left the remarkable possibility for non-death, except the tall building, which if he could have witnesses and 'slip' — oh, this was far too imprecise for him. In his suicide, he should, like an elegant equation, have a step-by-step plan that would allow for his ultimate solution. To balance it out, like an equation, where he was at last finally reduced to zero.

Chapter 7:
Heidegger and
Hardware

And then Joanne asked him to get the leaves and gunk out of the storm drains. She'd been asking him for a year, she reminded him, since the storms, and he still hadn't done it so would he please…

Of course. Yes, he was a year behind in cleaning out the storm drains, as if that mattered to anyone anywhere, least of all him, when he was a year behind in killing himself. Wait: As he walked through the hardware store, he realized what Joanne was unknowingly giving him. A solution. Here, before him, were literally hundreds of ways to die if he had the imagination to enact them. His hands lingered on the handle of an axe, the box of a drill, a huge length of rope and chain.

He stood there, staring at them, daydreaming, when

suddenly he was aware that the other occupant of the aisle — some shortish young woman in a bulky sweater — was waiting for him to make a move, to take the axe and move on. He turned and made eye contact.

The woman had impossible gold eyes. She gave him an awkward smile.

"Oh, I'm sorry," he said, "am I blocking you?"

"Oh, I just wanted to grab — "

"Go right ahead."

"I'm just looking, but I wanted to — "

"Please."

She motioned to move in front of him, and they bumped slightly.

"I'm so sorry!" he said, and "Oh no, it's fine," she murmured.

She paused, knelt down to pick up the 50-foot chain. She tugged on it, as if testing it. As she bent over, he couldn't help but notice her ass. He was not one of those type of guys who stared at ladies' cleavage or behinds (unless he was on the internet, of course) but hers was a perfect plum type shape. Firm but pronounced.

She turned back to him and caught him looking.

He was mortified.

She gave him a quick smile. "Do you use these?" she asked.

Use these? What, chains? "Uh... I haven't had the need for... uh... chains lately so..." He let out a small bark of a laugh. But where was the joke? God, he was stupid.

"I just thought since you were looking at them, you might be purchasing them."

"No, I'm actually here for a new ladder," he said. "My old ladder is a wooden one. It's rotting. And my wife..."

As he was saying it, he realized: Of course! He already had

the perfect tool for the job. A rotting ladder! He just needed to fall off the rotting ladder! It was so simple!

And of course, he was still there staring into those gold eyes, his own slightly glazed with the revelation of the ease of his impending end.

On the young lady's part she was having a pheromonal reaction. Bertie had been sweating, and profusely, walking into the hardware store. When they bumped into each other, she was breathing in deep, nervous about the chain she was getting for a three-way. It would be her first time using a chain, though not her first three-way. The smell of his sweat made a perfumed balm for her nerves. He had a sweet face, a funny face. A face like a stand-up comedian.

" — my wife thinks we need a new ladder, but I don't know." No, he didn't know. He didn't know he still had feelings that — what *was* he feeling?

"You don't know…?"

"Whether or not to get a new ladder."

"Oh, well, I'm not sure about the chain either," she said. She was losing confidence in the idea every second.

Neither of them were aware of the other's malignant purpose for their benign hardware, and both were sad to see the other's face downturn.

Mr. Snow's helpful, teacher-self prevailed. "How about this… I'll help you pick a chain, you help me pick a ladder?"

Her gold eyes immediately filled with hope. "Okay," she said.

"So what do you need the chain to do?" he asked.

The woman had this moment of searching for a lie, but she remembered the self-help book she was really into: Be impeccable with your word.

"I am going to chain up two guys. For a three-way S&M thing."

Bert swallowed.

He stared at this little librarian-assistant looking girl. He remembered his comedy improv training all the way back from his undergrad days:

Always say 'Yes, and…'

Saying 'No' gives the partner nowhere to go. Say "Yes, and…." *and you can create a world with your partner.*

He reached his hand out and touched a chain. This one was clunky and thick, like for pulling up a tree at the end of a tow truck.

This other one was thin. He wrapped it around his hand. This chain would leave marks, bore into the skin perhaps, but was light-weight.

"I think I'd prefer this one, personally," he said.

She pulled out a person's size length of the chain and held it up against her with a heave. "I agree," she said. "Let's go find you a good ladder."

The lights — fluorescents hanging from the ceiling — cast a magical Technicolor hue. The floor — concrete — seemed to bounce back. The Muzak version of "Don't Stop Believing" seemed like film score. Of course, it was terrible lighting. Of course, it was a terrible song and a terrible store, a terrible place to spend one's time, a level of bourgeois purgatory. But Bertie Snow found himself suddenly feeling as if he could happily remain in Al's Hardware for hours, years, forever.

His usual sense of paralyzing paranoia when being forced to talk to strangers, especially women, was absent, replaced with a not unpleasant sort of buzzing in his abdomen. His companion to the ladder aisle was someone with whom he felt an immediate sense of ease. She was not only attractive but obviously had a keen and absurd sense of humor: "A three-way S&M thing." Hilarious! And she continued to be an easy conversationalist as they stopped to discuss the differences between aluminum and wood and what height and weight of the ladder was most appropriate.

"This one," she said, settling on a fine silver stairway to heaven, "I think is the one. Aluminum, stretches out to 100 feet, *and* it's on sale for 20% off."

She had deemed it so, and so it was the one.

They walked to the checkout line. He insisted she go first. But as she was pulling out her card and paying he had a momentary panic:

Why did he let her go first? What sort of stupid chivalry was that? She was now going to leave, and as he flustered around trying to purchase this damned ladder, she would be gone and he wouldn't be able to —

"Thank you," she said to the checkout guy.

She flashed Bertie a smile. "Well," she said, muscling the chain around her to stick out her hand —

"Wait," he shocked himself by saying, "can I walk you to your car?"

She nodded.

The ladder purchase was beyond awkward. Apparently, it *was* on sale, but it didn't ring up as on sale, and then the young woman had to remind the checkout guy that it *was* on sale, and then the checkout guy had to send another worker to do a price check to ensure that it was indeed on sale, and —

"It's fine, don't worry about it," Bert said trying to grin through it. "I'll just pay what it rang up for."

"Oh, it will just take a minute," the young woman said.

"It's twenty three dollars! Just let him check — "

— and then the ringing and approach of another gangly teenage boy, and Bert's head now going full throttle — God, why did he ask this poor woman to wait for him? Surely she had better things to do than ensure some middle-aged man got his stupid discount — why wasn't he standing up for himself? She must think he was such a loser, wanting to walk her out to her car, insisting she go first, and then blubbering like an idiot over a discount, not able to stand up for himself, sweating in his stupid suit — God, he could smell himself, reeking of pathetic middle-aged man smell —

— finally finally finally the gangly teen came back. "Yep. It's 20% off."

"How do I ring up a discount?"

I want to shoot myself in the face, Bert thought. *I need to shoot myself in the face. I need to.*

He looked over at the young woman, who didn't look irritated at all. She was laughing, like it was some in-joke between the two of them. With a smile and half-shake of her head, she nudged him. They had an in-joke, now.

"Do you need help carrying that to your car?" the teen asked.

"No!" they said in unison.

"I'm sorry that took so long," he said to her, now out in the parking lot alongside her, trying to look cool while carrying a ladder.

"Oh, it's fine," she said. "I am fascinated by what happens to people when they are in ordinary aggravating circumstances. You can learn a lot about a person by what they do while they wait for something, or how they behave when they feel their time is being wasted. It's sort of my post-modern take on Heidegger's Theory of Anxiety describing the human condition, but I think in particular with modern society, it is less about the anxiety of death and more about the anxiety of having to wait for something — though in a way that feels like a death — the death of your time."

Did she just mention Heidegger? Yes, and she was still spouting philosophy.

" — As a culture, patience has lost its value. Everyone wants everything now. Actually, it's more like they want it to have already happened, like the time between wanting something and having it is nonexistent. There's this writer I like, Martin Amis, and he was talking about how he wanted to have another cigarette while he was smoking one. This is the modern condition of anxiety and death wish."

He had no idea who Martin Amis was, but he imagined if he had picked up smoking, smoking two at once might have accelerated the cancer. He tried to picture whether that might look cool.

When she spoke she had a very serious expression and she spoke quickly. A university student? Definitely, by the strident tone of someone accustomed to defending her opinions in class.

"I think it's what our society trains us to do — it's this constant cycle of creating false needs and desires and filling them at an ever-increasing enormous rate — so that they desire something — the pursuit of whatever it is, even something as mundane as a ladder, for instance — why if you could, would you not have just thought of it and then had it suddenly appear for you? Wouldn't you have done that? Just stayed home and snapped your fingers and made it appear?"

She stopped and looked at him, waiting for an answer. They were at a car now, he guessed hers, a small silver thing caked with dirt. No bumper stickers.

Oh, she was waiting for his answer. He wanted to agree with her, but he couldn't.

"No," he said.

"Really?" she asked, surprised. "Why not? You would have saved that whole trip and think of all you could have done with that time!"

"I wouldn't have met you, though."

She blushed, and then he blushed. And then they were both blushing.

He hadn't meant to flirt with her — he wasn't trying to flirt — he felt terrible now... he was a married man! He was flirting with a young college student who was enamored with Heidegger... what was wrong with him? He was leading her on! He was leading himself on! He was leading —

"Well, yes. It was the best trip to the hardware store I have ever had," she stammered.

"Yes — I... it's been a pleasure — you seem very...." He struggled to find an appropriate adjective. "Smart."

Her lip curled in a little. Was that the right thing to say?

She popped her trunk and threw the chain in.

"So, jokes aside," he said, "what's the chain for?"

She turned to him, her smile freezing. Then her face dropped. She turned back and closed her trunk with a soft shut. She turned to him again, her face calm and composed.

"It was a pleasure meeting you," she said. She did not offer her hand. She gave him a perfunctory smile. "Good luck with the ladder."

Seeing that she was clearly being polite and waiting for him to say goodbye, as well, confused as to what he had or hadn't said so obviously wrong, he could do nothing but say, "Yes, you too, very — "

She walked toward her driver's side door, and he stepped out of her way.

She drove away slowly and gave him a small wave. He waved back. He was clearly inept, as usual, but on this occasion he was mystified as to *how*. And as he watched her car drive away in the parking lot that became grayer by the moment, he realized he had forgotten to even ask her name.

Chapter 8:
The Sacred
"Yes, And..."

Missed opportunities can take on proportions far beyond their original possibility. His original thoughts about killing himself had been replaced with a new obsession:

How exactly did he kill a thrilling moment?

He had many theories. First of all, obviously he had come on too strong. He had been flirting with her — he a married man — and she had perceived it and been totally grossed out. But then, hadn't she blushed? Hadn't she said it was the greatest hardware store experience of her life? Hadn't she been flirting — if he had been flirting and not simply enjoying her company — right back?

He replayed every detail over and over in his head. Memorizing the gestures, the looks, the dialogue — trying to recall exactly, *exactly* where he had gone wrong.

If he were a younger man, he would have chalked it up to his unluckiness with women. But because he hadn't even been trying to get anything from her, because it was, above all, a friendly encounter — a human encounter — there was something about the entire thing that made him think that if he could figure out *how* he had screwed up, he would be able to figure out what was so screwed up with him.

Was it because he had said she was smart? Maybe it was that he couldn't follow up her long monologue on modern convenience with an appropriate addition. Maybe he seemed like a real dolt — she didn't know he was a mathematician, he hadn't volunteered that — so maybe she just assumed he was a non-conversing middle-aged suit, no one she could really talk to, and that moment was the moment when she knew finally, once and for all, that he was not her intellectual equal.

He wikipedia-ed Martin Amis, and even started reading him voraciously looking for clues. But he found nothing. He even wiki-ed Heidegger, and could understand less than nothing.

But his gut said it was because he had violated the sacred improv rule of *Yes, and…* His gut told him it was when she said what she needed the chain for, and he said, "Jokes aside…."

But it seemed so petty of her to let a small thing like his inability to reply properly to her comment make her react so violently, no not violently… *resignedly*… in the face of all this. What was she, some Groundlings/Second City/Upright Citizens Brigade improv rule fascist?

Maybe that was what she was used to — a smart girl in a world where even after a long heart-felt monologue about modern society, with allusions to German philosophers and British authors — and he, like every other man she met, could only state the obvious, calling her 'smart' and ruining her wit with his oafish comment and his inability to appreciate her humor, of all things, meant he was not a man to be considered any longer.

But it was only after a night spent fitful reading "Time's Arrow," and in his dream playing their scene in Al's Hardware again and again backwards and forwards in his mind, did the voice tell him the answer.

"*She wasn't joking.*"

She wasn't joking about the chain.

She wasn't joking about the chain!

He had betrayed her. He had hurt her. She had thought he was somebody who understood, and then at the last moment he had clearly revealed himself to be an utter disappointment. To die now without righting this situation would be to die worse than a loser. He must rectify this.

Not knowing her name, or anything about her, he went back to where they met.

Al's Hardware, which now had taken on proportions so beyond its function he almost wept in the parking lot.

An elderly man, a clear victim of 'not being able to retire and forced to do menial labor' was working the counter.

"Who was working here three days ago for the evening shift?" Bert asked.

The man doddered until Bert saw the gangly teen stacking some boxes. The one who had helped them.

"You!" said Bert. "Do you remember me?"

"Uh…," said the kid.

"I was here the other day and there was a young woman here, as well, and — I'm afraid she lost something in the parking lot" (*good one!*) "and I need to get it back to her. " (*Good thinking on your feet!*)

The Al's Hardware worker looked like he thought Bert was trying to con him.

"Do you remember?" Bert asked again, more desperately this time. "The young woman who — "

"No."

"There was a discount on the ladder. It took forever."

"If you want to leave something here for her, maybe she'll come back for it?"

Bert shifted his eyes this way and that. How different it all seemed now:

Here was reality! Shitty lighting, horrible concrete, migraine-inducing Muzak, gray, dull, ugly, soulless, detestable — everything he couldn't tolerate about stores, about America, about life!

He thrust his card to the manager in disgust.

"If she comes looking for it — just tell her to call me. It is too valuable," (*be polite, don't be an asshole, now, don't be one of those asshole pricks you hate*) "too valuable to leave."

He took out his card, which seemed so sad and stupid for this cause. A stupid card he had made ten years ago, back when he was still working the comedy circuit but keeping himself in pad thai by tutoring kids in mathematics. It was a sad little gray card with a younger version of his face as a variable in the point-slope formula that read, *Bert Snow, tutor of high-level mathematics.* He was embarrassed to still have it, more embarrassed that he would actually leave it.

"Do you have a pen?" Bert asked. The worker had to

go back to the counter, dig through the drawer — God, everything in this place took an inexorable amount of time! — but finally a pen was found for him to borrow.

Bert wrote neatly on the back of his card:

You helped me with the ladder. Please call me about the chain.

He didn't kiss it, but he said as close to a prayer as he, an atheist, could muster in his mind. *Please, let me find her again.*

And he handed over this only hope for his heart to this uninspiring manifestation who muttered, "If someone asks, I'll give her this."

The someone never came asking. But he would later find out her name. She was, of course, Dominique Colt, who in two years would be famous for two of the most brutal murders of white boys in the history of Los Angeles county.

PART TWO

Chapter 9: Psycho-Bitch Killer Whore

Two years prior to becoming synonymous with "Psycho-Bitch Killer Whore," Dominique Colt had just been a graduate student in love.

Felix, before he was a man who'd had his head bashed in by a decorative brick that said "LOVE NEVER FAILS," was a writer in the process of getting an 'in' to writing for television with such staggering speed it was amazing that he was still working as a checkout guy at Green Grocer's.

Dominique was getting her Master's in Clinical and Social Psychology at Southern California University, Reseda (SCUR). SCUR had a solid Master's Program in Psychology. It prided itself on semi-competitive admissions, and rigorous academics. Dominique was working on her thesis, which hypothesized that modern depression and alienation stemmed from a lack of meaningful social groupings.

The broadness of her topic was now her major hurdle and the chair of her committee, a Dumbledore-type, albeit with shorter beard and an endless assortment of brown and green cardigans rather than wizard robes, strongly advised her to do a case study on a particular social group. And if Dr. Philip Goldstein suggested it, he who was Dr. Freud, Socrates and God the Father to Dominique's mind, it would be so.

He suggested a cancer-treatment support group.

Dominique pretended this was immediately of interest and that she would look right into it, but at age 23 she was bored with the idea of cancer.

Dr. Goldstein, when he made the suggestion, was unaware that cancer was currently beginning a quiet get together in his pancreas that would quickly erupt into the party that would end his life in four short months.

Dominique would have immediately followed up on Goldstein's lead, interesting or no, but she had a date with Felix at her apartment, a semi-depressing chattel cage called grad-housing just off the Reseda campus. She had a roommate named Georgia (who would give her aforementioned murder weapon/decorative rock as an engagement gift), a Religious Studies student who tended to stay in her room with the TV on making Dominique and Felix feel like they were alone in the apartment.

Dominique was head over heels in love with Felix, who had a mop of curly hair, a kind of dumpy boy body, and a tattoo on his upper arm of Felix the Cat. Felix was gregarious and easy to talk to, and so interesting. He had things to say about almost everything. He was intensely political — a vegan, an environmentalist, and an arm-chair politico. He could tell you everything that was wrong with everything. He had these 'monologues,' as she thought of them privately, that he saved for the appropriate plug and play. These monologues were anecdotes of funny and interesting things that had happened to him, conspiracy theories, obscure movies he'd seen and books he'd read.

He seemed graceful in all of the ways she wasn't. And more over, not repressed in the ways she was. Whereas she had a vague sense of embarrassment about things like oral sex, he was eager, adventurous and normalizing, like there was nothing weird or wrong about having one's face in another person's privates slobbering all over them.

After one year, Dominique was still eager to please Felix in whatever ways she could, to keep secret that he was her first real boyfriend, to keep buried deep just how lame her life had been up until the point that she had met him. They kept talking about moving in together, but it hadn't happened yet.

It had been almost a week since they had last seen each other. They were both pretty busy, she with school, he with working and writing. Plus, he had just joined a band. He was going to be playing the keyboard with a group called Flight Detector that he was forming with some guys from work.

So they went into her small bedroom, and he plugged his phone into her speakers to play his playlist of Death Cab for Cutie and Arcade Fire, and they started making out.

She was always happy when that awkward moment between not kissing — knowing you were going to — and kissing happened. She was always glad that he took care of making that whole routine play out.

She was faintly bored as he gripped the back of her head

and moaned, his tongue insisting she unclench her teeth.

Which she did.

In went his tongue into her mouth, and his hand started on the outside of her gray t-shirt with a silk-screened Frieda Kahlo face on it. Frieda's eyeballs were on Dominique's left breast, and Felix was moving his fingers around and into those eyeballs.

This was their routine. When they saw each other, before anything, before they went to the movies, or before they went for a walk to the store, or before they listened to music, or before they smoked pot, whatever they were going to do as they "hung out," they would have sex. Felix had verbalized this as his preference, so he wasn't thinking about it all the time they were together. Then, they could always do it again if he slept over, or she slept over, or do it again in the morning.

She had only had sex once before Felix, with a fellow member of the Speech and Debate club, and that guy was too drunk to stay hard (or maybe she was just that unappealing, God she hoped not) and the penetration had been painful and awkward and she had insisted he put on a condom, which he tried to do, then lost his erection, and rolled over and went to sleep and snored so loudly she had picked up her clothes and skulked out of the room.

She had really liked that guy, Paul, had fantasized it would be like sleeping with Darcy from "Pride and Prejudice" because he was so full of pride and liked to tease her, even though, or probably because of the fact that, she beat him so soundly in the Lincoln/Douglas debate. After that night, she and Paul had never talked about it again, though part of her ached for him to say it "meant something" to him. He never did, and so she supposed it would just have to mean something solely to her. Dominique often marveled at the irony that in Jane Austen's time, a woman's virginity was her most cherished commodity to be safe-guarded and protected, and how now most ladies saw it as something to lose as quickly as possible, an embarrassment to keep.

Her roommate Georgia was still a virgin because, somehow, she felt she wanted something special, and yet she was also constantly mortified by the idea of it. Dominique could offer her no consolation. She did feel intense relief, if not superiority at having her own be gone and enjoying regular sex. Well, enjoying was the wrong word for it.

Tolerating.

Dominique was very much in her head, couldn't have an orgasm. At least, she hadn't yet. The truth was, when she perceived that Felix was getting frustrated or his jaw was getting sore, or she had just had enough of the whole sort of alarming experience of a man slurping between her legs, she would begin a performance. She would imitate what she had seen in movies, what porn she had seen, she would roll her eyes back in her head and say, "Oh, yeah! Oh yeah, yeah, yeah! Mmmmm! Yeah!" until she had reached a sufficient pitch in her voice and then she would sort of shudder and pull herself away.

She was lying, she knew, but she didn't want Felix to feel like all that work had gone to waste, and she did love him very deeply and did want him to continue to be her boyfriend.

So now Frieda's face was crumpled on the floor and Dominique was in her dingy, white bra (she knew she had to go to Victoria's Secret or something and get better underwear — it was just so expensive!) and Felix was fingering her. It was a little painful but she was moaning like it was the greatest thing ever.

And then he stopped. He pulled his finger out of her, looked off into space, and said something very surprising:

"I think I might be gay."

Dominique knew plenty of people who were gay, and none of them seemed to enjoy sex with women as much as Felix did — or have had as much sex with women as Felix had. Felix knew this, and he began his monologue.

He'd been feeling a little bored with sex with her (Dominique) and he'd been thinking about other women (he didn't apologize or seem to feel guilty about it) but then on the first night of rehearsal with Flight Detector, they'd gotten drunk and Jim, who played lead guitar, and he had loitered around, and then Jim, while they were talking, just casually slid his hand down the back of his pants and fingered his asshole. He was surprised, and he'd liked it. And since then, well, after every rehearsal, the two of them had stayed late, and well, they were now having anal sex.

Dominique knew that the appropriate response to this was probably to feel betrayed, to start crying, to order him out of her life and to begin therapy immediately, and being in training to become a therapist herself, she could certainly find someone to help her on a sliding scale. But she found herself, instead, fascinated by Felix's story.

And proud of him, in a strange way, that he was brave enough to embrace a homosexual encounter with the same openness he engaged with the world, and to accept it so totally and completely that he didn't even pause at the possibilities that he may be bi-sexual, or just someone who wanted anal stimulation, or that this was just a gay affair, but went straight to thinking he was gay.

So Dominique, who usually did very little of the talking,

found herself, in her still wet and gray underthings, giving her own monologue steeped in loving and compassionate wisdom. He shouldn't judge himself in totality by this one affair and if he also enjoyed sex with women and was simply bored with the current state of his relationship, then perhaps he had more exploring to do before he labeled himself as gay or straight. He was a human being, and human beings are complicated, especially in matters of the heart.

And after Dominique's short but beautiful monologue, Felix began looking at Dominique with wonderment, like she had suddenly appeared before him, new and more desirable than ever before. And he suddenly attacked her, ravaging her, grabbing her by the back of the hair, tearing her bra down so her breasts were exposed.

He nestled his face in her breasts, and then he started to cry. Felix gave big wracking, kid-sized sobs, how confused he was — and how he knew she loved him, and he loved her, too, but that he didn't know what to do — what were they going to do? Should they break up? What should happen? How could he know what to do and-and-and what now?

She kissed him and consoled him. She felt as tender as a mother, as sweet as an angel. She kissed his tears away. She told him she loved him. She told him she would stick with him. She said she wanted him to be true to himself, and she would help him do that.

And then he begged her to put her finger into his asshole.

Dominique was grossed out.

First of all, his ass was kind of hairy.

Second of all, it was his rectum. Where poo came out. And given that Felix was a hairy man, and that poo did at certain times come out of there, Dominique was aware that she was very likely going to get poo on her finger.

And that was gross.

But he was begging, and she loved him.

So be it.

Felix bent over the bed. And everything in her mind shifted to a world of just him, pleasing him, his sensation, he this animal, she this tool for his pleasure. And then, some time between her inserting not just one, but then two and then three fingers deep into his rectum...

She finally, and completely, came to orgasm.

Chapter 10:
The Proposal

At the next Flight Detector show, Dominique was particularly aware of Jim, the guitar player. Maybe it was because he didn't meet her gaze or catch her eyes, but acted like she didn't exist at all. Dominique could only assume he knew that she and Felix had rekindled their love life and was jealous.

Since their last encounter, Felix had talked about moving in together. They seldom spent a night apart. And he was coming home from band rehearsal — proof, in Dominique's estimation, that her assumptions were correct and that Felix was not gay, only someone who liked anal stimulation.

Jim, on the other hand, she now knew, despite his hetero-posturing, was most certainly gay and probably in love with Felix. His peevish, obvious jealousy confirmed that.

But Dominique refused to be petty and she kept trying to smile at him, make polite gestures, and cheer loudly when he played his solos. After the show was over, Felix was pulling down his equipment when Jim saddled up to her.

"You want a drink?" he asked.

Now, that was generous indeed!

Dominique wasn't a drinker, actually, but she said 'yes' and asked for a beer. Felix, glancing towards them and seeing that Jim was playing nice, flashed Dominique a smile. He hadn't brought Jim up since that night, but she knew that he wanted everyone to get along.

Jim returned with the beer but gave it to her with a grimace, like she had pulled his arm out of his socket to get it.

"I'll always buy a pretty woman a drink," he said.

Dominique was about to say 'thanks' when he added, "Or an ugly one who's easy."

Dominique wasn't sure what that meant. Was he calling her ugly? She certainly wasn't ugly. Perhaps you could call her 'plain,' but she knew she wasn't 'ugly,' and she certainly wasn't going to take the bait.

So she drank the beer. "Good show," Dominique said, gamely.

"Oh, it sucked," Jim said. "We totally blew on that last song."

"I couldn't tell," Dominique offered.

Jim shrugged. Then he walked away.

The evening spiraled into Dominique hanging out with the band until the bar closed. The lead singer, Eddie, invited them all back to his place. Dominique fully expected Felix would want to go to Eddie's, but he shrugged and said he was tired.

Felix had been bringing different types of toys home to experiment with, and the last one, a long plastic banana that hummed and could actually peel, was something he seemed pretty excited about.

Dominique couldn't help but notice the deflated sack Jim's

body became when Felix said he was tired.

It was just like Dominique to be sucker enough to feel guilty about making a guy feel sad, a guy who tried to steal her boyfriend and who insinuated she was ugly. She couldn't help it, though. She was a psychologist in training, hyper-aware of others' feelings.

As they drove back to her place, Dominique brought it up.

"I think Jim feels rejected," she said.

"He's fine," said Felix.

"I think he really likes you and is disappointed that — you know — we're, you know, staying together."

"He's gay, I'm not. He has to get over it."

But then, the next week, Felix had a new idea on how to help Jim.

"Hey, Dominique, I was talking to Jim. He kind of confided in me that... I dunno. He isn't gay. He likes girls. He just, well, maybe he's like me."

"Hmm, that's interesting," said Dominique, knowing better.

"What would you think about... having a three-way with us?"

Dominique had heard of such things, but the hearing of it didn't go far in her imagination. It seemed like complicated geometry, like a game of Twister. She had never liked the game Twister. Well, she had never played the game Twister because she was so sure she wouldn't like it. She had certainly never considered it as something that would happen in her life... to her.

"I don't know about that," she said.

Felix started to beg. "Please," he said, "if you could give me this present, I swear, whatever you ask of me... I will do. I will marry you."

Dominique was confused. Did he just say, "marry"?

And then Felix was suddenly on his knee, his brown, soulful eyes wet with emotion, looking up at her. "Dominique Colt, you are the most amazing, sexy, sweet, smart, and kind human being I have ever met. You excite me, you fulfill me, you make all my dreams come true. Will you marry me?"

Dominique couldn't help but start crying, she had never expected this. She had hoped, maybe somewhere, someday, maybe in her subconscious that she and Felix might...

"Yes! Oh Yes!" she said, conveniently forgetting that she was, with this acceptance, also tacitly agreeing to a three-way.

She called her family. First her mom, then her sister, then her dad. Her mother and sister squealed with delight. Her mother talked about how much she liked Felix, her sister talked about whether she or Georgia would be maid of honor.

"Can't I have two?" Dominique asked. Her sister assured her that no, she would have to choose between her best friend for life who was also her sister and some girl she had met two years ago who was intruding on their relationship.

Her dad, a vague presence since her parents divorced when she was eight, seemed to think she was shaking him down for cash and kept asking about what kind of wedding she was expecting.

She then told Georgia, who assumed she would be maid of honor and immediately started talking about planning the bachelorette party.

When Dominique told them all there wasn't a date yet, everyone kept pressing her to get one and soon. It was more pressure than finding a college or declaring a major. And in many ways, Dominique felt that it was implied that this was more important than college or her major, or grad school for that matter.

A man loved her enough to marry her! To declare her his, in front of God and everyone, to be faithful to her for life!

Chapter 11:
The Dominique-trix

They didn't need a date. It happened all on its own.

There was a Flight Detector gig at the Spot Bar in North Hollywood. Dominique's semi-precious ring caught the stage lights. She felt pretty. She felt loved. And she had to admit, honestly, that Flight Detector was beginning to sound better. She was dancing, unlike the bar's other four patrons who barely even looked up or managed to clap.

During their song, "You're the One," Felix sang from the keyboards the harmony, "Oh baby, you know it, you know it so well, you're the one!"

It was a stupid kind of song that sounded like every other song, but there was something about it that night that got her.

Maybe it was the way Jim launched into his solo — like it was a weapon, like he was drawing blood. Felix had said fairly regularly, "I think Jim is a musical genius!" Dominique doubted this, but nodded to be supportive. But tonight, there was no doubt he was something.

Jim looked right at her — his fingers moving across the guitar — and she suddenly, for the first time, felt a little excited about their agreement. Felix didn't seem to notice — he was usually high as a kite, eyes closed, as he played keyboards. Jim's solo even made the other four patrons look up, and at the end of the song, give sincere applause.

Before the band had even packed up, Jim left his guitar. He made a straight line toward her. Jim, it should be known, looked a little like the latest guy they cast to play Superman plus a few choice tattoos and a mean glint in his eye. He worked out. He wasn't dumpy or doughy or cute. He was hot.

So when he walked toward Dominique like a tiger going for the kill, she was prepared to submit as an antelope to such an obviously superior creature.

But he didn't rip her jugular out, he just said, "What are you and your *fiancé* doing tonight?"

Dominique shrugged.

Jim mockingly shrugged back. He got close to her ear. "You want two cocks tonight?"

The way he said it, she kind of thought she might.

They thought about going back to Dominique's place, which she considered a bad idea, seeing as how Georgia may be home with her eagerness at discussing the wedding. So Jim offered his.

Jim lived in a small bachelor pad in Eagle Rock. Felix was either incredibly high or nervous or both. He couldn't shut up, he just kept talking and telling stupid anecdotes she knew both of them had heard a hundred times.

" — Which is why I am pretty sure the post-record

company movement is going to revolutionize the industry and propel music making to new heights — "

(*Shut Up!*)

If Jim were actually straight, she would ditch Felix for Jim in a heartbeat (*Stop it, that's not true*).

Jim flipped on the light. His place was covered with psychedelic posters, Jimi Hendrix, Janis Joplin, Miles Davis. Everything in it was either hot or cool. He had a record player. He put on Ray Charles.

Felix didn't touch Dominique, not to hold her hand or put an arm on her. Felix was thus, she realized, also in his mind wondering if Jim were perhaps the more appealing offer.

Jim locked the door. The music was loud, and there was something disconcerting about the brass of the band, the strength of the voice, after all the emo music she'd been hearing.

They all stared at each other for a moment.

"Can we get stoned?" Felix asked with his best *Oh, if it wouldn't be too much trouble* face.

"Sure," said Jim. They sat on Jim's orange couch.

"I like this couch," Dominique said.

"Found it on the street," Jim said, condescending as always, like everything she said was the height of stupidity.

He packed a bowl.

"You know the movie 'Last Tango in Paris'?" Felix began, and Dominique knew this monologue led to the conclusion that Marlon Brando revolutionized acting, but that the subtext was butter.

Dominique decided it would be best to make sure they were all on the same page. "I think we should all be clear about what our boundaries are, what we are willing to do and not do."

Jim looked at her with his same *Oh my God, I can't believe you just said something so stupid* expression and laughed.

Felix laughed, too.

The bowl came to her. "No, we need to know what our lines are. None of us have ever done this before, right?"

"As far as you know," Jim said with an eye waggle that let her know her assumption was definitely correct.

So Dominique found herself in the role of organizer of the Twister game as preferences began slowly spilling out. Jim really wanted to be tied up, and he wanted Felix to have anal sex with him. They both suggested tying up Dominique and giving her anal sex, popping her 'anal cherry' they said, but she was not interested.

"That's because you've never had it," Jim said, and Felix agreed.

"I don't care, I don't want it and that's that."

"What if we tie you up?" Jim said, like it was a threat.

"Yeah, what if we tie you up?" Felix chirped.

"I don't want to be tied up at all," she said.

Felix smoked-coughed at the same time. "Uh- I've never uh- done that. Been tied up."

"You'll like it," Jim said.

"Tied with what, though?" Felix asked, a worried expression creeping on his face.

Jim undid his belt and pulled it through the belt loops. There was something about the way he did it that made Dominique feel the first pang of arousal.

He handed the belt to her. The feel of the leather, the studs in it. The firmness of the material. Her hands moved over it, stopped at each stud as if it was sharp, though it wasn't.

"You can even hit me with it, if I'm bad," Jim said. His eyes had incredibly long lashes, very black, and his eyes were the type of blue that, with his pupils dilated as they were right now, looked like a dying sun in the… what phase was it when a star died and turned blue? Blue dwarf?

"All right, then," Jim said to her. "You're in charge."

"I'm in charge?" she said, touching the buckle now.

"Well, you are the Dominique-trix," Jim said.

"Oh, that's genius!" Felix said between helpless giggles.

She had forgotten for a second that Dominique was even her name. Maybe she was just that high.

"I'll be the Dominique-trix," she repeated.

Jim gave her a smile that was nearly shy. "Should we get started?" he asked her. "There's something I've been hoping you'd do for me," he added in a low voice that made her feel like she might do anything for him.

"Yeah, what's that?"

"Felix tells me you have a way with assholes."

Dominique blushed, laughed. Felix laughed. They all laughed a little too much. Jim undid his pants and slid them to the ground. He wasn't wearing underwear.

His penis was flaccid. And huge. He bent down on all fours. He pushed a shiny pink asterisk at them both.

"Um," said Dominique softly, unsure what to do.

Felix started giggling nervously. Hysterically.

"Baby, it isn't going to lick itself." That Jim was calling her 'Baby,' which frankly, no man had ever called her, and was asking her in a low throaty way to lick his rectum was alarming, no matter how high she was.

Dominique did not find this sexy. Not at all.

"Please baby, please. Please baby, please…" He waggled his bottom at her like an eager puppy. "Put that tongue in it."

Dominique looked back at Felix. He gave her an earnest nod.

This is what it took to get married?

So be it.

Dominique bent down. Jim's butt, though it did have a few zits, was pretty chiseled. It wasn't hairy, like Felix's, which she had never licked. It was a nice butt. The kind of butt they'd have in male underwear ads.

Jim stopped saying anything. It was up to her. She was in charge.

She swallowed and brought her face closer — sticking her tongue out —

And then the pink hole clenched and released a noxious gas right into her face.

He'd farted on her.

And then Jim jumped up, clapping his hands and laughing, his penis flapping like it was in on the joke. Felix was laughing as well, like this was some sort of candid camera moment they'd set up for her.

Dominique felt the pit of her stomach drop out, and she realized she might burst into tears. Jim's face was so gleeful, so victorious, that she didn't realize she had slapped him, and hard, until she saw a bright red welt blooming on his cheek.

He stopped laughing, bringing his own hand gently to his face.

Dominique grabbed his penis in her hand and twisted.

Jim screamed in pain.

"Get down on your knees," she ordered, her face hot. She was going to twist it off for all she cared.

"Oh my God *stop* — *please* — *stop* — HELP!" Jim looked like he might puke his guts out, faint or both, and gag to death on his own vomit and die like a 70s rock star.

Felix rushed over to her with a limp whine, "What are you doing? You're hurting him!"

"Back off, Felix!" she growled.

"But you're — "

"BACK OFF!" She turned her face to his, her face contorted like an angry golem. He had never seen his sweetie like that. Actually, he had never seen her angry before, at all.

Jim crumpled down to his knees.

And in the downward movement his penis slipped from her hands.

He was on his knees in front of her, cradling his penis and kind of leaning into her at the same time.

Felix went to his knees as well, with a really annoying, "Are you okay? Are you okay?" for Jim.

But Jim was leaned up against her hips, his breath hot against her as he moaned in pain.

"Felix, his penis hurts. Make it better."

Felix looked up at her with surprise.

"Kiss it and make it better," she commanded.

"I don't want to do that," Felix stammered.

Dominique grabbed him by the hair. "You didn't say that before, Felix." And she pulled his head down to Jim's crotch.

She grabbed Jim's belt from the couch. "And I think you should perform cunnilingus on me now, Jim," she added.

Jim gave her a look of sheer terror that showed he was genuinely disgusted by the thought.

She grabbed the belt, looped it in her hand, and whipped it hard against his bottom. He thrust out with his pelvis with the hit. Jim's penis was only slightly erect, but when Dominique slapped him with the belt again, it got more so.

"Take Jim's penis into your mouth," Dominique ordered Felix.

Dominique knew he didn't want to perform fellatio —

he'd told her that a million times — but he hadn't set it as a boundary so that was just too bad for him.

She bent down and bound Felix's hands with Jim's belt. He could get out of it easily, but she could see Jim's penis stiffening as he watched Felix being bound.

"Suck his cock," she ordered, finding words he might better understand. Felix clamped down his jaw. "DO IT!" she commanded, with a voice from her own throat she'd never heard before.

Jim guided Felix's head, tenderly, his fingers in his curly brown mop like he'd loved him forever and always.

She'd remembered to wear nicer underwear. She'd shaved for the occasion. She might as well try. She unzipped her jeans and pulled down her own underwear, feeling like she was some other person entirely. She was an Amazon woman, a 50 ft. woman. She was a woman who took all pleasure into herself.

"Now you lick me off until I come," she said to Jim, and straddling poor Felix who sounded like he was choking, she pushed Jim's face into her.

Jim was still on his knees.

They were a weird triangle now, with Felix's head beneath Dominique's legs, kissing Jim's penis, while she decided to make use of whatever groans of pleasure Jim was having by thrusting her vagina onto his face. She knew it was repulsive to him. She didn't care. It made it better, in fact. So much better — a power surged through — everything that was once shame burning off of her — to force someone — not just someone, *Jim,* on his knees to her, doing something he found revolting, disgusting, but he was doing it *good good good* to her — *for* her and —

Jim had an orgasm and Dominique had an orgasm, and Felix had nothing but a mouth full of fluid. He couldn't help feeling cheated, especially by a conspiratorial gleam he caught between the two of them, as if they had planned to leave him out in someway, as if they had planned to make him doubt everything.

Felix spit Jim's fluid from his mouth onto the ground. "Uh, um, I still need to get off," he said, easily slipping the belt off his wrists and actually raising his hand like he was in school.

Dominique snapped back quickly from whatever cloud she was on to this world, which was all about Felix.

"Oh, I'm so sorry!" Dominique said.

"My bad!" said Jim, as he tried to get erect enough to give Felix anal pleasure, but he needed more time to get it up again, so he ended up manually stimulating him while Dominique agreeably squeezed her breasts together and pressed them into Felix's line of vision. But even as Dominique seemed impressed with Jim's technique, Felix felt his hands were too rough, too fast, too sure of what they were doing. Sure, he came, but it was predictable.

And then that was over, and they got dressed and laid around listening to Hendrix, getting high.

It seemed Felix's idea had been the right one, after all. This was all it took. Look at them: Dominique and Jim got along swimmingly, now. They laughed at each other's jokes, kept giving each other shy glances. Felix sucked in another bong rip. He'd been the bridge between them. And he'd seen a side of his fiancée he'd never seen before.

Felix had initially hoped that Dominique would be the female bridge for his homo-exploration, but watching the two steal looks from each other, Felix started to suspect he was the bridge for Jim's hetero-exploration. And Felix didn't really like being the bridge. And Dominique was something else entirely. Making him suck cock? Tying him up? Forgetting about him? When Felix talked about it, later, he always told it with great effect, thoroughly enjoying being the sexually liberated male with a wild nympho fiancée and best friend who were both in love with him and completely all about pleasuring him. But immediately following the act, it was a real drag. Ass sore, jaw sore, and no one interested in anything he had to say.

Two holes and a spigot.

It got him off, but it really wasn't all that much fun.

So he said:

"That was so awesome, you guys. I really think we should do this again."

On the car ride home, Dominique felt strange. On one hand, it was very interesting that her Id, her animal nature, had come to her rescue. Nothing like that had ever happened before. Up to this point in her life, in tough situations, she would cave in and cry if need be, but here, she stood up for herself. So she was proud of herself, in that way. And she had made her own pleasure a priority, which was good, too. And she had become this other person, a woman who ordered men around, who told them what to do sexually, who slapped them and hurt them. She had been in control. She was not used to feeling in control. That control felt good, like she was playing a character, and the character was someone she wanted to play again in the near future. It was good.

What was not so good was this vague feeling of weightless sludge in her belly, like she was both sick and full, and sick and hungry at the same time. What was not good was the cloud over Felix's head and that worse than that, she didn't really care all that much if it was there or not. She was already blaming him in her mind: this was *his* idea, *his* friend, and now *he* didn't like it? Each time he said "how awesome that was" he sounded more disappointed. But she was too busy thinking of something else.

In her own mind, a movie was playing consisting only of close-ups of Jim: His face as he handed her the belt, his voice when he named her the Dominique-trix, his face twisted and determined as he held her clitoris between his perfect pouty lips, which were red and slightly chapped.

She had never kissed him on that mouth.

And she wanted to. She really wanted to.

Chapter 12:
The Hole

Dr. Goldstein was known for his dynamic lectures, with his rapid-fire ideas that either blew the brains of his students or made them angry at his priggish assuredness. His Psychology of Religion class was one of the most popular classes in the department because he wove together elements of pop culture, Marxist theory and media criticism. He would talk about movie stars as the current saints. He'd compare Marilyn Monroe to Mary Magdalene.

"These stars are our saints. We visit their altars on the screen, and with the price of admission we show who we worship."

Dominique ate it up like an All You Can Eat buffet.

"It is important to understand," he'd say, a light twinkling in his Dumbledore-eyes, waiting with a dramatic pause, "that for a culture, religion is the system made by those in power and practiced by the participants of the society, enacted through their daily rituals *regardless of belief.*"

Students would nod (or nod off, depending on the time of day of the class) trying to grasp the meaning of these concepts as he strung them together like abstract music with notes only certain ears could hear.

"The national religion of America is this thing called money and the market is how money moves. This is an idea, really, but practically forced participation is how the society enacts itself. Trading things for an agreed upon idea of something called value.

"The dream is to be utterly taken care of, held by money, so that life becomes an endless comfort, an endless beach filled with endless sex objects and intoxicants. The nightmare is to be the person who waits on the pampered, the unseen who refills the lotion bottles, who cleans the plates, who bleaches the towels, who works day in and day out. The dream is to be the consumer, the nightmare is to be consumed. The dream is to be the phallus. The nightmare is to be the hole."

It had been a rollercoaster of three weeks since Dominique had last met with Dr. Goldstein, and when his name popped up in an email, it was with a nightmarish feeling that she realized she hadn't followed up on the cancer support group. But worse was this prickling in her mind that said he knew somehow what had had her so tied up as of late, her participation in the ménage-a-trois, that Unholy Trinity, that had tainted her, making her unfit for the life of the mind.

He was in his office, and when she knocked he actually got up out of his chair to hug her. She felt shame rush through her. He, of course, didn't know. He thought she was the same person she had been three weeks ago. And here she was, about to deceive him.

"I haven't had a chance to put together the thesis proposal yet," she said. "I just got engaged."

"Congratulations!" he said, as if it were genuinely good news. "That's wonderful!"

"Yes!" she chirped.

"It's fine about your thesis proposal. Actually, I am going to need to ask you to find another chair of your committee. Please… it's nothing personal."

In an instant, Dominique thought in detail of every personal thing it could have been that resulted in this, her life flashing before her eyes and culminating with her fingers in someone's rectum.

"I need to take medical leave," he said.

"Oh," she said, relieved it wasn't about her. "Are you okay?" A stupid question considering what he had just told her.

He gave her a smile. "I'm not sure," he lied.

As she walked back across campus, her phone rang with a number she didn't recognize.

It was Jim. He asked if he could meet her alone.

They went to a restaurant Felix would never go to. A place called *Everything with Bacon*. Jim ordered Bacon pancakes and Dominique stuck to a BLT. Jim didn't make a lot of conversation, which was fine. Dominique was used to Felix talking constantly, and it was kind of nice to just sit and be in a place without having to have a comment on it.

Things had definitely changed.

Jim was looking at her with something like love. She wasn't sure that was it, since she had only really seen it with Felix after she started the anal penetration, but it was definitely now on Jim's face, too.

Jim talked shyly about growing up in the Midwest. He talked about his first band, Free Beer, which was a name that totally backfired on them.

Dominique talked about her thesis, about the kind of practice she wanted to enter into. She didn't mention her wedding. Neither did he.

He paid for their meal, insisted upon it. As they walked out, Dominique felt it was best to straight up ask. "Did you like being slapped?"

Jim thought. Then he nodded. "I didn't like it when you screwed with my junk though. Please don't do that again."

"Don't fart in my face, and I won't."

He smiled, revealing perfectly straight, white teeth and a slightly crooked lip. "I'm real sorry about that," he said. "That was a real shitty thing for me to do, but I gotta tell you… I think I've been in love with Felix and really jealous of you."

Well, duh.

"And now?" she asked.

"I think I'm over that. But now it's something else about you. I wanna figure out what that is. You make me feel… I don't know. Weird. But good."

She looked at him, holding that intense blue gaze. Weird, but good. Yes. A sensation of being seen for a part of herself she hadn't known she'd had. Of being something stranger, more powerful than she'd ever thought she could be.

Then he invited her back to his place to get high.

She and Jim walked down the street, nearly holding hands, but not quite. They wandered into vintage shops, they got ice cream. And they passed a turret that seemed attached to

nothing at all. On a wooden door there was a sign:
Those Who Accept Not Death May Enter
"Oh wow, what's this?" giggled Dominique.
And they went inside.

It was a bit like entering into another realm. It was 79 degrees outside, bright beyond bright, and this place was as cold and dark as Christ's tomb. A high-ceiling marble antechamber, where crushed black-velvet curtains hung, so no one could be the wiser if it were day or night. The place looked a bit like a movie set for a cookie-cutter Count's castle. On a budget.

Jim and Dominique shared a look.

"Spooky," Jim said with a wink.

A pale woman at a desk about twenty feet from the door was staring at them both with a rictus smile. Jim turned to Dominique to whisper something catty and suddenly the woman was right before them.

Jim jumped.

"Do not be frightened," the woman hissed. "Though The Order may be intimidating, one should enter with courage."

Jim laughed. Dominique tried to be more polite. "We just saw the sign and thought we would come in." She picked up a pamphlet and began reading.

"And you will be forever grateful for that curiosity," the woman said. Her accent was a strange mix of Southern California Valley and something Eastern European. The woman had bleached blonde hair pulled up into a peak, enormous, firm breasts, stick-like legs and very plump red lips.

"Oh, you're the fake vampires," Jim said loudly, rudely,

with a comical head-slap like he was remembering a joke.

The woman seemed offended and a bit intimidated by Jim, though she wasn't letting on. "We are fake nothing!" she said with sudden venom. "Vampires are *real*."

Dominique was fascinated with the pamphlet:

𝕿𝖍𝖊 𝕮𝖍𝖚𝖗𝖈𝖍 𝖔𝖋 𝖙𝖍𝖊 𝕴𝖒𝖒𝖔𝖗𝖙𝖆𝖑 𝕺𝖗𝖉𝖊𝖗

The Church of the Immortal Order is the only true Vampiric Order with members who are actual Vampires. Every other vampyric sect is populated by posturers who will die.

The Church of the Immortal Order is a secret, sacred Order. Our membership is secret, but does include some of the highest ranking political officials, celebrities, as well as many strong Vampires posing as ordinary humans.

Dominique stopped reading, Jim was tugging at her.

"Hey, let's get out of here," Jim said. The woman was staring at him with a hungry look. "Go smoke some pot," he added.

Dominique nodded, stuffing pamphlets into her purse, thinking she might have found something far more interesting for her thesis than a cancer support group.

"'Vampires are real,'" Jim imitated, in a mocking tone as he threw his weight into the wooden door and made it rock on its hinges. "Real, my ass."

Chapter 13:
Nymphomaniac

Once Upon a Time, before brutally murdering him, Dominique believed in having open communication with Felix.

"I had lunch with Jim," she told him, as he was lightly tweaking her nipples.

"Oh, that's cool."

"Yeah, I think he and I could become friends."

"So you wanna do the three-some again?" Felix asked, with a bored expression.

Dominique shrugged. "You said that *you* did."

"Yeah, it was pretty good, I guess, but I dunno."

"Okay."

"Yeah. I'm really stoned right now," he said.

"Okay."

"But yeah, we'll do it again."

Then he turned over on his side, away from her.

She missed the next Flight Detector show because she had a test the next day. She stared at the open textbooks, with a paper to write, never mind her thesis. She needed to focus. Maybe she could work it out over the summer. Her student loan payment had come in. She was now 60,000 in debt.

But she didn't get any work done that night.

Felix came over, with Jim. It was the first time Jim was in her place, and she felt suddenly exposed. Luckily Georgia wasn't home, she was at a conference on religion and culture in Palm Springs, and Dominique explained several times that the decor in the common area — obviously mind-numbingly bourgeois — was all from Georgia's parents home. Dominique whisked them as quickly as possible into her own small room.

Jim seemed impressed with her books, her papers everywhere. He asked questions about her studies and her preparations for her thesis. Felix asked if Jim had a joint. He did. They all smoked pot.

Dominique had something to share. She had a chain she'd bought from the hardware store. Jim looked at it, appraising, and rewarded her with a smile that made her blush.

"Let's put it to work," Jim said.

And Dominique slowly, but firmly began to give directions.

She didn't want it to be too loud, because even though Georgia was gone, there were the neighbors to consider. She fashioned some gags.

She gagged them both, her hands trembling with excitement as she placed it over Jim's chapped lips.

And the encore performance of the Dominique-trix began.

It was even more exciting, with the roles more defined and the movements better orchestrated than the first time, even in her little cramped room.

And then Felix said suddenly, easily moving the gag out of his mouth: "You know what… I'm kinda over this."

"Oh?" said Dominique.

"Oh," said Jim.

Felix was over more than the three-some, apparently. Whenever Dominique and Felix met up, Felix was tired. Felix wasn't feeling well. Felix had a lot of work to do. And even having sex with her seemed to weird him out. It stopped being the first thing they did before actually hanging out. Felix would just fall asleep. And he didn't even mention the wedding anymore.

After a two-week stint filled with halted conversations in which Felix only talked about his ideas about culture and politics, Dominique suggested maybe they should take a break while she worked on her thesis for the next month.

Felix actually sighed with relief.

Meanwhile, she and Jim had lunch every day.

The flirtation and the connection between them was so electric, Dominique found herself wondering if she had been mistaken. Perhaps he was bi-sexual. Perhaps there could be a way in which the two of them had an even deeper relationship than being part of a triangle with Felix.

And then on a Tuesday, Jim surprised her by bringing a guy with him to lunch.

"Dave," the guy said to her, upon introduction, with a handshake so firm she winced. He had a close-cropped haircut, and was lean and built. Dave was a black belt in Tae Kwan Do. He was in law school. He was a big fan of Jim's guitar playing. Dave played the sax and wanted to start a band. Dave had a cock-sure every-boy swagger with Jim, but with

Dominique he was polite, sweet, gentlemanly. He looked at her like she were some stunningly beautiful woman, which was not part of Dominique's usual experience.

Then she found out why.

"Jim tells me you are some sort of..." (she was waiting for 'nerd' or a more polite version of that) "...uh, *nymphomaniac*."

Jim gave Dominique a wink and then proceeded to, over their pesto and chicken paninis, proposition Dave into a three-way with them. Jim had apparently built up these grand tales of Dominique's sexual prowess to Dave, who, curious as any hot-blooded 24 year old, type-A boy would be of sex without strings, agreed to experiment with them. But he said right from the start that he was freaked out, sort of, so for starters, he just wanted to watch what Jim and Dominique did.

Dominique, from the moment Dave said the 'n' word, had been unable to properly jettison herself into character, for she was completely unfamiliar with what role Jim had cast her as.

So she just did the best she could to agree and be agreeable, which seemed to win her adulation from both of the very attractive men.

And then she was back at Jim's, with this guy named Dave, and they were all taking off their clothes, with Jim whispering cues to Dominique about how to be the Dominique-trix he had hyped.

Jim made a performance of having sex with Dominique, which he was clearly faking his way through, then as he lost his erection he looked to Dominique to save him.

"Suck it," Dominique instructed Dave.

"No, *you* suck it," he fired back.

Jim looked at Dominique, waiting for her to slap Dave or tell him that *she* called the shots, not him. But she couldn't find it in her to do it. She didn't really know Dave, and she didn't want to make him uncomfortable or upset.

Shrugging, she performed oral sex on Jim, who again made a show, and then turned to Dave.

"Now let me do it to you," Jim said.

"I want her to do it," Dave said.

"Tie him up," Jim whispered to Dominique. She knew he thought it might be easier for him to get to perform oral sex on Dave if he were tied up.

Dominique complied with her best commanding voice. "Put out your arms, I am going to tie them!"

Dave laughed at her. "Nah. That's not for me."

Jim gave him an insistent stare. "No man, it's good."

Dave shrugged. "Then let me see you do it first."

So Dominique tied up Jim. As soon as Jim was securely tied, Dave surprised them both.

"Now I want you to watch," Dave said to Jim, and he grabbed Dominique, lifted her up, put her legs around his pelvis and copulated with her so vigorously and intensely, his whole body a paroxysm of work and pleasure inside her, that she felt her body shudder with a sense like destiny, rescue, completion, purpose, fulfillment, forever — this is what it meant to be truly completely —

And then he pulled out and came all over her face.

He held her a moment, then turned to Jim.

"Lick it off," he said to him.

The next day, Jim was understandably pissed off at Dominique.

"You didn't DO it right," he told her, over lunch, barely

touching his food. "You aren't supposed to let him call the shots. You're the Dominique-trix. How could you forget that?"

But she was feeling surprisingly very over Jim, and annoyed at his peevish tone. She couldn't make someone gay for him. Certainly not someone as aggro-hetero as Dave.

For Dave had messaged her on Facebook, asking if he could call her: *I think you're incredible and your boyfriend is gay. I'm not. Wanna try a straight guy?*

Dominique did not think about Felix first, but Jim. She didn't want to betray him. But....

"But what do I do about this?" she said, relating the FB post.

Jim looked at her like he might throw something in her face. Something sharp. "Are you fucking kidding me?"

But Dominique was already mid-blue fairy-tale fantasy of Dave being her prince, and she being some Cinderella and the perfect fit wasn't about a slipper but his rock hard —

"Oh, fuck you," Jim said. And he stood up and walked out.

Dominique sat for a moment, alone with her half-eaten Caesar salad and Jim's abandoned salmon burger. She looked at Dave's profile pic and wrote three letters quickly: "*Yes.*"

But when her phone beeped again it wasn't Dave. It was a message from Georgia. She was just texting to say how sorry she was about Dr. Goldstein.

And that's how Dominique found out her mentor was dead.

Chapter 14:
The Natural Enemy
of Vampires

"Do you even know how much it costs to make a realistic version of a severed windpipe?" The question hangs in the air of Casa Vega. No one attempts to answer, and Madeline, who asked it more rhetorically anyway, decides to just leave it there.

They are all a few drinks in (well, Pussy sticks with the Perrier — she is sharp, Mads should watch her back around this one) and they are at the *let's re-cap what we've learned* portion of the evening. When the bill comes, no one looks at it for a full twenty minutes. Finally, the waiter comes by and says, "I'm leaving my shift, but whenever you are ready," and everyone looks non-committal. The one who gets the bill is the one who is being granted the favor.

It is a silent face-off between Pussy and Madeline, but it is Julian, on whom Pussy bestows a "Of course, Julian should get a 'Producer' credit, and thank you so much for introducing us!" who finally takes the bill like he'd been planning to all along and would hear of nothing else.

Madeline walks back to her car.

It has been a long lunch at Casa Vega. It is January in L.A. and a positively chilly 62 degrees and the sun is already setting. Madeline has had to street-park at Casa Vega, she can't afford the valet, and as she walks she looks at her phone, liking posts with reckless abandon.

She drives the mile home as the sun winks goodbye and she parks on the street. She walks toward the small shack above a garage that is her apartment and sees that there are two men, dressed all in black, outside of her place.

What are they doing, just standing there?

She walks toward them. As they see her, they turn and start to walk away.

"Hey!" she yells at them.

They bolt, jumping down the stairs and running down the street. Now Mads is really scared. She is one of the Xs on a headshot, she knows it! She goes inside and locks her door, sticking a chair against it for good measure and trying to find some forgotten garlic she might have somewhere. Only garlic *powder*. Shit!

She thinks about George Clooney. What if he were the Master, if he wanted to suck her throat — would she allow him to make her one of his cronies? She pictures him, looking at her with that look of his and his crinkly forehead.

"I know, Mads," he says, "I know this is strange but, I want us to be together, really be together," which is pretty good but not as good as if he were a Vampire Killer and trying to enlist her to help him, his hand touching hers as he explains the mission is too dangerous and how she would insist and then in case they don't come back alive…

…and then she masturbates.

She doesn't turn the lights off to sleep.

She falls into a fitful sleep with dreams, again, that Dieter is floating outside her window.

She has those re-occurring ones that are the worst, where she wakes up — oh it was just a dream — she opens her window — wait, Dieter is now walking outside — wait he's floating — wait, she wakes up — no that was a dream too — so that by the time it is actually day again she is bleary and when she sees Dieter huddled in a shadow near her front door, she hopes to wake up again.

"I braved the sunlight for you," he says.

"It's fucking southern California. If you don't like sun, move to Forks."

He flinches a little with that, but pretends he doesn't get the reference. "Madeline, I think we need to talk."

"Dieter," she says, with her best/worst Colonel Klink accent, "stop calling me Madeline, first of all." She now finds a serious adult tone. "Second, you need to go to Vampire rehab or something."

He puts a hand out towards her and makes a slow circular swoop, like he's casting a spell. "You don't believe immortality is possible, Madeline?"

She mocks his hand gesture but betters it with an extended

middle finger that lands upright. "No. I guess I don't. I think you are with a bunch of sick fuckwads who have hard-ons for Dungeons and Dragons."

The Deets she used to know would have relented with a giggling fit. But this shade of a Künstwerk is quick to anger. "You are judging me — and them! — with no evidence. Nothing. You still know nothing about it."

"Dieter, you were about three seconds from fucking biting me."

"No, I wasn't."

"Bullshit."

"I would never bite you without permission, Madeline. But I do want you to understand everything about it. I want you to join me."

"Do you know how fucking crazy you sound right now? Join you? In what? Not eating? Having weird plastic surgery? Hanging out in the dark? Dieter, I fucking love the sun! And I'm a vegan! You think I'm gonna drink blood?"

Dieter puts on a hang-dog expression. Mads feels bad for him. Deets is the type of guy who couldn't convince his best friends to see a movie with him they are 'meh' about seeing, how the hell does he think he would ever convince someone to be his immortal beloved?

"Can I come in?"

Mads knows movies. "Is it a vampire thing?"

"Whaddya mean?"

"That's a vampire thing. Once I invite you in, you can come in anytime you want, right?"

Defeated again.

"Fine, forget it, Mads," Dieter says, and turns around, the sunlight already turning his fish-belly white skin red even in just the three blocks he has to walk back to the only parking space he could find in the neighborhood.

"Fucking street parking," he hisses as he walks away.

Madeline half expects him to desiccate and blow away right there as she watches the speck of him recede from her window, a poor white thing burning in the light.

Madeline knows who she is. She is self-interested and self-aggrandizing. She is a genius, sure, but she is the only one who really knows it — for now. And letting everyone else in on that truth must always be her first priority. However, she is also a human being with feelings, and she is interested in the welfare of her friends and doesn't want them to wither away and die as self-delusional Vampires.

So Madeline gets herself a stiff drink (there was coffee in it, too) and asks herself a hard question. Who could help Dieter?

She can't. Sure, she is a genius, but she is no match for a bunch of Vampires. Maybe George Clooney could do it, but he is busy playing basketball with Barack Obama and not taking her calls.

There is only one group she knows that are the natural enemy of all Vampires. One group who might take the case:

The Christians.

Chapter 15:
John Lee is on a
Mission for Christ!

A Bi-racial (Asian, African-American), beautiful bodybuilder with a voice like a tenor saxophone and an IQ of 132, John Lee is destined for greatness.

But there is no greatness but through God! John Lee has been witnessing since he was a child, and there is one thing he has been certain of his whole life long.

Jesus is Lord!

John Lee, just 26 years old, is the founder of the Cross-Fire Church, based out of Northridge and serving the California State University, Northridge (CSUN) campus and San Fernando Valley Community. Cross-Firers are similar to many other evangelical Christian sects in their literal interpretation of the Bible, their poorly drawn pamphlets condemning nonbelievers to Hell, and their belief in salvation by grace rather than works. They are *different* from other Christian sects in that they are sworn to destroy the Vampires. This is why Madeline has sought out John Lee, in particular, to help her with her Vampire infestation. This is why she needs John Lee.

But John Lee says, "It's not about John Lee. It's about Jesus Christ, and the message the world has to hear."

Madeline tries not to yawn. "Look," she says, "I think the world got the message an Inquisition ago, okay?"

She has offended John Lee, who starts this whole long talk about how Catholicism is a 'whoredom of Satan' and Madeline tries to listen politely and widen her eyes appropriately because she is wondering if he can help her with the fucking Vampires or not.

"UGH!" she finally yells out to stop him. "Look! I'm not here to talk about the Catholics. I want to know if you can help my friend get away from the Vampires! He's not converting to Catholicism, he's in the middle of this whole fucking thing where they are doing weird surgeries and taking weird supplements and I don't even know what shit — "

"Please don't curse."

"Huh?"

"We believe in keeping the mind, body, and language clean."

Madeline refrains from calling him 'a fucking idiot,' and instead gives a terse apology. Geniuses should be self-serving, though many fall into the trap of self-sabotage. She will accomplish what she sets out to do. She will help Dieter.

Because he is her friend.

And because she is as scared *of* him as she is *for* him.

Madeline details how she believes Dieter has gotten messed up with the Vampires: Secret "Twilight" obsession, post-German-Hitler-guilt/fascination, general shifty-little-fuck, probably recruited easily as a new bottom for their pyramid scheme…

John Lee bears a look of concern.

"How little you understand the Vampires and how they feast upon the unsuspecting souls they convert to everlasting hell!" he says, brightly.

"Okay, so can you help him or what?"

"Yes! Of course!" John Lee says. "Christians are natural enemies of Vampires! We have many natural enemies, of course, but none so newly pernicious as the Vampires. We at the Cross-Fire Church specialize in fighting Vampires. However, they are a recognized 501(c), Nonprofit Organization protected by the United States government. Therefore, we don't drive stakes through their hearts — at least, not until the Second Coming. What we do is engage with them on a dogmatic level, actively disagreeing with their — "

"Wait — " Mads cuts him off. "You fight them by *disagreeing* with them? Frankly, I need something a little bit more persuasive."

John Lee takes a deep breath. "The best thing you could do, Madeline, is to convert to Cross-Fire Church and then actively work with him, as his friend, to change his mind."

Madeline smacks her hand down on the table.

"I don't fucking need you to disagree with him and try and change his mind, I need a fucking cross and some fucking fire of God type of shit, like your fucking Cross-Fire name! Now, do you do that or are you all just talk? Because I can get the fucking *talking* part from every Christian denomination right down to the fucking Unitarians. If you specialize in it, you better have something fucking special."

John Lee crosses his arms.

"Do you believe Jesus Christ is your personal Lord and Saviour?"

"Uh, no," Mads says.

He shakes his head.

"You can't help me if I don't believe what *you* believe?" she asks. "What does belief have to do with it?"

And John Lee stands up, like the conversation is over, and Madeline feels a panic coming on. In two hours it would be night and she would be back to attempting couch surfing with people she'd not returned calls to or emails from in six months.

"John Lee, listen. I need help. My friend has red fucking — I am sorry... *freaking* — red *freaking* eyes. He is getting botulism injected into his forehead. He is stalking me and sending others to stalk me. He needs help. I need help. Please. Help. Me." She is near tears. Madeline doesn't cry in front of people. No no no.

John Lee takes pity on her pain. He takes the golden cross from around his neck and puts it on the table in front of her. "Here," he says. "Put it on."

Sniffling, but not yet crying, Madeline puts the cross on around her neck. She feels a little weird about it. Technically, she is part-Jewish somewhere, but she figures that given the circumstances, it couldn't hurt.

"I'll tell you what," John Lee says. "If you will bring him to me, I'll do my best."

"Your best what?"

John Lee sighs. "You'll see," he says.

Madeline calls Dieter at midnight. He picks up. She can hear the drone of voices in the background.

"Hey, I figured you were up, since this is your new five pm," she says.

"I'm somewhere important, Madeline," he says. "If you will let me mind-meld with you, I can show you this place, but cellular technology is not appropriate."

"Deets, will you meet me at the In-and-Out on Cahuenga?"

There is a pause. "Why?" he asks.

Madeline feels bad about it, but not as bad as she would've thought. "Because I want to try and understand you, and if you'll meet me, I'll consider what you have to say… if you will consider what I have to say."

"I'll be there in ten minutes," he says, and hangs up. And then she knows that, even though he is totally gay, Dieter actually loves her.

John Lee, outside her window, looks expectant. She gives him a thumbs-up sign. Then he goes and sits in his car across the busy parking lot.

The In-and-Out glows like a promise.

Not long after, Dieter pulls up next to Madeline's car and sees that she's eating fries. Dieter opens her car door and gets in. He sniffs the air like a bloodhound.

"I braved meat for you," she says, calling back to his 'braving sunlight' statement. He gets the callback and nearly smiles. "I got you a double-double animal style," she adds patting the untouched burger that rests near the parking brake. "You hungry?"

He shakes his head, but his red eyes say better.

"Your Vampire buddies have been all over me," she says. "I

think giving them all my info is a pretty low blow."

Dieter shrugs. "I've given them *all* of my contact information. Everybody I know or have ever known."

"That is so creepy."

He looks at her mildly. "They are Vampires, Madeline. Creepy is the least of your concern."

"I called the Christians on you," she says.

"*Which* Christians?" he asks.

"Does it matter?"

"Why'd you do that?"

"I'm sick of the fucking Vampires, Dieter. And I'm sick of you not being able to eat. And I'm trying to be a good friend."

And John Lee raps on the window.

Dieter turns his face to see the beautiful vision of a man and immediately rolls down the window.

"Hi!" says John. "I'm on a mission from Christ, can we talk a moment?"

Dieter rolls his window back up.

"Listen," Madeline says. "You told me you wanted out. This guy has an offer for you,"

"It's a Cross-fuck," he sneers. "You brought in those Cross-fucks?"

"They call themselves 'Cross-*Fire*,'" she corrects him.

"Do you know what they *do* to Vampires?"

"Annoy you?"

And John Lee climbs in the backseat, and Madeline starts driving before Dieter can escape.

And John Lee starts talking. "Dieter Künstwerk! You are on a path to eternal Hell!"

Dieter groans. Madeline feels like groaning, herself.

"You have been led astray by the evil one to lust after blood, when the blood of Christ is the only blood that redeems!"

Her cool friend Deets turns into Vampire-acolyte Dieter, a nasty hissing thing that spews Vampire-speak. "No!" Dieter snarls. "Once the Master returns, I will gorge on blood — like yours! For eternity!"

"Dieter, it is the grace of God through the sacrifice of our Lord Jesus Christ that is what allows for eternal life, that and that alone!"

"Wrong!" Dieter hisses. "I will never die! I will live forever under the dark wings of my Master!"

"Then you will be preserving yourself, in your sin, for all eternity!"

"I care not for sin. Sin is a petty human constraint!"

"Do you not see that the body, flesh, is merely the coil for spiritual truth? To preserve your body in sin is Hell and Damnation!"

"Better to reign in Hell than serve in Heaven!"

"Dieter, think! This is eternity we are talking about — forever!"

"No!" Madeline butts in. She can't take it anymore. "We're not talking about forever, we are talking about right now!"

They both look at her as if *she's* the crazy one.

"Nobody *wants* to die, that's not the point," Madeline says. "This isn't about *not* dying! This is about how you *live* your life! And the Vampires are simply brainwashing their members to think that not dying is a possibility, just like the Christians with their whole resurrection thing!"

Dieter gives her a look. "But beloved, immortality is what is at stake here."

"Your eternal soul," continues John Lee.

"Wait, this isn't about me," Madeline reminds them both.

"Of course, it is!" they say, in unison.

The car is now outside No Bar on Magnolia, and she slams on the brakes. She gets out of the car and slams the door behind her, leaving Dieter and John where they are. They can steal her car, for all she cares. She's going to the bar.

Here she is — when she could be trying to find additional financing for her movie, doing her stupid re-writes or writing a new movie, or doing anything, actually — and she is having some bullshit intervention for her fucked up friend. Well, let him be a Vampire. And let the Christians be the Christians. They could all just fuck themselves forever, for all she cares. She just wants them to leave her out of it.

They don't follow her in, thank God for small miracles. She is crying a little, she is surprised to find. The blonde tatted bartender asks her what she wants. She orders Anejo tequila, neat. The Cranberries are singing "Zombie" on the juke-box.

She doesn't get it. She has never needed to join anything, to be part of anything. Well, wait. What about Hollywood? What is it that she *wants* with this movie? She wants people to acknowledge her work as an auteur filmmaker. She wants people to know she is a genius. People like… George Clooney. Is Hollywood, thus, her religion? Her delusion? Could it be…?

Nah.

She finishes her tequila and puts it on the card (minimum payments only until she gets famous and can pay it off).

When she walks outside, both occupants are now in the backseat. John Lee is holding Dieter, who is sobbing. On Dieter's cheek is a dark red smear, like a misshapen mole. He has cried out his red contacts.

Madeline never finds out what John Lee did to Dieter. She asks John later and he says, "the power of Christ compelled your friend's immortal soul to open, and he had to deny the evil Master," but Madeline suspects that a powerful and immediate crush on the good-looking Lee might have had more to do with it.

Dieter is going to spend the next few days at Lee's home, with other Cross-Firers, 'de-toxing.' Dieter doesn't say anything to Madeline as he gets out of the car, but gives her a touch on the arm and a genuine, tearful, "thank you."

It is wonderful to see his eyes again, their usual dark blue.

Three days later, Dieter calls and asks Madeline to pick him up at Lee's place.

He looks really good. Clearly, he's been eating. His forehead is still unnaturally blank but she supposes three days wouldn't be enough time to bring back his characteristic eyebrow creases.

"I'm gonna have to quit Flashy," Dieter says, as they drive.

Madeline, who made lots of contacts through him and his job at Flashy Talent Agency, tries to hide her disappointment. "Really?" she asks casually.

"Yeah. I think I'm gonna go home for a while and try to sort stuff out."

"Home?"

"Back to Germany. Just hang out with my mom and... I dunno... lay low for a while."

Dieter is a true-blue transplant Angeleno. He'd never, ever wanted to leave. The sun, the traffic, the palm trees, and the ordinary-ness of a day in Los Angeles — they are soaking in it. To decide to go back to Germany...

"Deets, are you really *that* scared of the Vampires?"

Dieter smiles at her. His tooth is still filed to a point.

"Yeah," he says. "I am." Then he looks out the window, a sad expression on his face.

She opens the glove compartment as she's driving, which is not a smart move, and she swerves some and misses hitting another car. She pulls the gold cross out.

"Lee gave me this," she says, "to protect me against you. You can have it now, to protect you against them."

He holds the cross for a moment. And then with a sigh, he puts the cross around his neck and looks out the window. "I had a chance to be a Vampire, a real Vampire. Instead, I got saved by Jesus, just like a million other losers."

Chapter 16:
Old Star, New Acolyte

Meanwhile, somewhere in Brentwood — where twenty years prior, Ron and Nicole had moved on to their eternal reward — Cecilu Harris is unhappy with her new face.

She doesn't want to admit it to herself, but now when she looks in the mirror, she feels a very strange sense of alienation. Whereas before she had felt a familiar sort of disdain in her thoughts for her reflection, like one would unleash on an envied sibling: *God your nose is so big! Look at that zit! You're getting so fat! Ugh, it's a wonder you have any friends, etc.*

Now when she looks in the mirror she is at a loss to think anything. She is merely startled and jumps back —

"Who is *that*?"

She has gone a little overboard. People had told her to go easy. Do one thing, just one thing first, but she had always had a penchant for dramatic changes. If she was going to buy new clothes she wanted a whole new wardrobe. If she was going to change the boyfriend, she would change the apartment, the pets, and heck, even the car. This sort of personality had earned her a reputation as a minor celebrity. She was a former sitcom star, trying to get her star to rise once more. She was hot, sure — she wouldn't be a TV star without being hot — but she wasn't pretty.

Her mouth was too small and pursed. Her nose too large and angled. Her chin too soft, her cheekbones too low, her ears too large. Oh… and her tits too small.

She wanted to feel like a new person.

So she had it all done at once.

And she didn't feel new at all. She was the same old person she had been, she just didn't recognize herself anymore.

Neither did anyone else.

Getting work became a problem. She had the Jennifer Grey syndrome — you change the feature people make fun of, that you think will make you beautiful, and maybe it does or maybe it doesn't, but whatever it does, nobody can recognize you so you don't get the roles that the big-nosed babe in Dirty Dancing would get.

But then it got worse.

But the time she hit thirty, she was already realizing that she had a less than human look. Sure, she didn't have wrinkles, but her face was pulled in a way that looked strange, menacing. And then, the only direction to go was more.

She has just had more plumping done to her lips and cheeks.

She has a bag of frozen vegetables on her face.

And now, with peas and carrots pressed to her cheeks, she listens to Vince.

She wouldn't be considering the Vampire route if Vince

Vaughn weren't so convincing. The thing about Vince is, he's a real charmer. And now that he is a Vampire, he is even more so. She once had thought of him as a sort of loser comedy buddy movie guy, but look at him, fooling them all. A real Vampire.

"Look, baby," says Vince Vaughn. "I'm not gonna tell you what to do here, I'm not gonna insult your intelligence like that, Cecilu. But you don't look good. No one else may tell you that, but I will. You fucked up your face."

Cecilu starts crying. "I am trying to fix it, I am trying to," she says, pulling off the veggies and letting him see her tears, which used to be moving to some.

"You can't unfuck it, baby" he says, sagely.

She starts to wail a little.

"But here's the thing, baby," he says. "You may look bad for a woman, but you look great for a Vampire."

Vince drives his 2014 Aston Martin — a small car for such a tall man — with the top down in the L.A. sunshine, Cecilu's check for $10,000 smackers in his back pocket. He is thinking of how many Juice Boxes he can get for that. He is thinking of his next movie role. He is thinking it is a shame he doesn't have an Oscar. He is thinking he needs his agent to start finding him some more dramatic roles. Show his range.

He is thinking again about Juice Boxes. Juice Boxes with long legs and big tits. Juice boxes who are just barely legal. Juice Boxes of every color and flavor. He is thinking of one with doe-brown eyes and knees that slightly knock. He is thinking of her neck. He doesn't have fangs (fangs are for the BS nubes) so she will come to him pre-pierced, her brown eyes all pupil, high as a rat on the honor of being his personal Box.

Vince gets a chub just thinking about it. He pulls into the Souplantation where he is meeting the Assistant to the Assistant to the Master. The Assistant to the Assistant to the Master fucking loves Souplantation for some unknown reason.

Vince sits down at a booth.

The Assistant to the Assistant to the Master is slurping minestrone soup.

"Hey," says Vince, taking out the check. "Got another down payment on Juice Boxes. And a new C class starter."

The Assistant to the Assistant to the Master looks up from his soup with a smile that would curdle the dreams of children in a twelve-mile radius.

"That's lovely, Vincent," the Assistant to the Assistant to the Master says. "Just wonderful." He touches Vince's arm with his white, smooth hand. A shudder goes through Vince.

"I need you to do something for me, Vincent," says the Assistant to the Assistant to the Master. "Normally, I would never ask you for something like this, but this is something I want you to handle, personally."

"Sure, sure," says Vince. "Whatever you need."

"It's just a little bug on the C track that needs squashing. But I'd like there to be a personal touch. Send a message."

"Can I get an extra Juice Box as a cherry?"

"Baby," says the Assistant to the Assistant to the Master, in a violin-strings-scratching-a-chalk-board imitation of Vince's Vaughn's own slang, "I'll get you twenty."

Chapter 17: The Changes

Madeline's fingers are flying furiously. She is sending over new dialogue to Pussy Foot, as fast as one can tax genius, when her phone rings with "Walk Like a Man" (the ring tone she had chosen for Foot which she is now thinking should be "Rat in a Cage").

"Madeline," Pussy says in her Carolina drawl, which for all of its honey stings Madeline's ear. "You wanna go fish for Clooney at the regular spot while we talk about the changes?"

The Changes.

Pussy is late, and when she arrives, she immediately starts in about the philosophy Mads has added, per her request.

Sweet as a butterscotch candy with a nail in it, Pussy purrs, "Now, you're a great writer and you obviously know how to get some real complex ideas into this story, and I think that is so incredible. It's why I love your story, but I think maybe you're still too far off from what this character needs to be."

Madeline stiffens, bristles, stiffens, bristles, bristle-stiffens.

"I appreciate what you're saying Pussy," she lies.

"Oh, why don't you call me Patricia, Madeline," Pussy says. "Let's talk to each other, woman to woman, and drop these artificial barriers between us."

"Okay, Patricia, but I am not sure exactly what your note is and what changes you are requesting."

Pussy smiles and takes out the The Changes that Mads sent her, changes to her precious, precious work.

"Do you hear my voice now, when you write her words? Do you picture me saying them?"

"I picture the character saying the words, Patricia. Not you."

"Well, listen then," Pussy says and reads, sans accent, with earnest effort:

DOMINIQUE

I am fascinated by what happens to people when they are in ordinary, aggravating circumstances. You can learn a lot about a person by what they do while they wait for something, or how they behave when they feel their time is being wasted. It's sort of my post-modern take on Heidegger's theory of anxiety describing the human condition, but I think in particular with modern society it is less about the anxiety of death and more about the anxiety of having to wait for something- though in a way that feels like a death — the death of your time —

"I mean, it's clunky, isn't it?" Pussy asks sweetly, her full accent back.

"You wanted her to sound smart," Madeline says, with a pained and forced smile.

"Oh yes, absolutely… but I don't want her to sound like she isn't real."

Madeline bites back some very elitist, derogatory things she might have said about Pussy's collegiate experience, or lack thereof. Instead, she keeps it professional.

"Well, that is your job as the actress, to sell it as real, Patricia. That is what makes a star a star." She smiles then, a bit too brightly.

Pussy considers it, then nods. "You know what, Madeline. I think there might be something to this. Maybe this 'death of time,' this wasting of her love and this anxiety is the key to her motivation."

"Sure," Madeline says. "If that helps you, to think of it that way."

"I think it does, now. And I hope I haven't offended you."

"I'm not offended," Mads lies, again.

"I'm so glad. But I hope you have really considered all the variables and varieties… about what you're doing here." She says it like a fucking psychic, like a woman about to read Mads' fucking palm.

Oh God, George Clooney! Please appear and save me!

"What am I doing here?" Madeline asks, mainly to herself, but aloud.

Bait taken, albeit hesitantly, Pussy pulls the line and hard. "Right now, you are re-creating the past, and that's sacred work. So you have to be careful because at any moment, you might have accidentally defined your destiny."

Um… what?

And then Pussy launches into a long boring story about her childhood in North Carolina — something about catching catfish and it never being the same river twice, and how each time she tells the story it changes a little. The drawl of Pussy's voice is hypnotic and soothing and it's the story you could fall asleep to, and Madeline is forgetting it as fast as Pussy is telling it to her. She doesn't have time for boring childhood stories. She's not Pussy's shrink, thank God.

"But I tell you this for a reason," Pussy finishes.

Uh-oh. "Why?" Madeline asks.

"Because I think you already know this, but time doesn't really work like that anyway." Her southern drawl makes Mads' skin crawl up her back.

Mads turns back to her with a what-the-fuck kind of look. "Huh to the what now?" Mads asks.

"Well, I think that time is more like a spiral," Pussy answers — but it sounds like, *'wehll, I think thaht tahm is moyhe lieke a spy-rahl'* – so Mads has to really piece that shit together.

Mads does her best to give her a thoughtful, considering expression. "How so?" she asks, thinking what a fucking idiot is sitting across from her.

"We feel time like it's a line," Pussy says, "like this and then this and then this, but one's mind is always going back and forth — thinking about the past — planning for the future — back and forth in time and then you are re-creating what happened in the past and fantasizing what will happen in the future — like I was saying about how we caught those catfish, but I don't really remember which time it was that we caught which fish, or if it was two or five times, and who was with me, my Cousin Bo or my Cousin Craig or both, and when it was that I stepped in the mud and felt it between my toes, which time was *that* — but *that* time was a golden moment — but where did that happen exactly?" (said 'eggs-acht-leigh').

Madeline stares at her. She is cold tripping right now because as Pussy is talking she is actually seeing it now, the pieces of Pussy's story she wasn't listening to. She is seeing Pussy, then called "Pats," age 7, with her little brown legs and her feet, still perfect though smaller and callused and dirty from running around barefoot "'ahll tha dem time.'" Mads sees them down by the lake. Was it Cousin Bo or Craig? And Pats' foot being in that mud and her looking down at her foot and feeling it — feeling every bit of sensation from that mud "sqoooushing in-between mah toes and feelin' a sense of pleasurah" that keyed her into a sense of destiny.

Something so simple as mud between her toes when she was 7, and she has gone back and forth to this moment so many times — this moment defines her *now* — this moment tells her who she *is* — a fulfillment of a childhood understanding that there is something transcendental in all of life, even down to one's toes.

"So I'm just saying you're already playing with what happened, why not play more — why not make it something nobody expects — not just the story of a killer... but the story of love?"

Mads downs the rest of her margarita, which is way too sweet.

"I'm sorry," Mads says, "but do you actually know *anything* about the real case? This woman chained up two guys and slowly bludgeoned one to death and slit the other's throat. Anger. Resentment. Revenge. Madness. But I wouldn't call it anything like Love."

Pussy gives her that grin. "Well, that's what takes a little effort then, isn't it Madeline? Finding love where others can't."

Madeline heaves a deep sigh. 50K with a guarantee of 150 more or not, this may be a deal-breaker.

"So use the Mystery Man," Pussy says.

Madeline gives Pussy a *whatcha talkin' bout Willis?* expression. Nobody touches her Mystery Man. It's the role she wrote for George Clooney, for Christ's sake!

But Pussy doesn't know when to stop:

"There's something bigger there than what you got. A big, invisible elephant in the room that is bigger than anything, bigger even than… George Clooney." And Pussy laughs.

WHAT? Is this woman high?

"That person could be *anyone*," Pussy says, "and whoever that Mystery Man was — he's not saying and she's not saying — and if that's not love…" And then Pussy bends in closer with a whisper like a secret. "…I'm sure no one would be the wiser if you called it so."

Mads can smell her lotion, she can smell her skin, she can smell her hair gel. Everything about Pussy Foot smells like sweet butter, and there is something heady in her, something that makes Mads understand why the men come to her just for foot jobs and pay her handsomely for that, why this woman has 50K to throw at her — and that this woman is also appealing to her sense of power — that she sees Madeline's authority, she wants something from her — and that maybe that something is something that Mads wants, too. That something is a thought, the mystery, an idea waiting to be born, bigger than anything she's ever conceived. Yes, even bigger than… the man she is waiting for. Even bigger than Clooney.

Madeline has to take a breath.

"You're a brilliant writer, Madeline," Pussy continues. "But

I think you could write something that's *genius*."

Madeline trembles. Pussy just said the magic word.

"And anyone who *can* do something *genius...*," Pussy says, dropping her voice low and bringing her lips in closer to Mads' ear, close enough to kiss her, "...really *should*. Don't you think?"

Yes. But who is bigger than Clooney?

PART THREE

Chapter 18:
Snow Gets Off

Late one night, Mr. Snow told himself stories about what would happen:

He told himself she would come back, that girl from the hardware store would call. He would take her firmly in his arms, he would tell her he never meant to judge her. He would ask her to chain him up, or he would chain her up if she preferred. He had never been chained up or tied up or any sort of kinky anything so he supposed he should give it a try.

So what had started as a human connection had devolved now, and had become all about the plum shape of her ass and his playing the scene differently:

Yes, she chained him up right there and then in the aisle... but then the teenage boy who worked there might come over and see them and so... no, in the parking lot then, yes the parking lot. But then he started thinking about the cars going in and out of the lot, and that might be more dangerous, especially if he were chained up, and what about that ladder? Oh God, he still hadn't cleaned out the storm drains! No good, no good at all...

He needed help.

He sat with the laptop, holding his dick in his hand, looking at the girls with their face turned in some "ooooh" expression and their eyelids half closed, pretending they were cheerleaders or horny housewives, and he would pretend he couldn't see himself in front of the computer, fondling himself and thinking of the girl in the hardware store, or the girl at the coffee shop, or what was most forbidden, a student. What student? Well... that Madeline Hunter, yes... she never shut up and now he was putting porn words in *her* mouth... yes, wait, how young is she? She's a senior so... she's eighteen, or seventeen? But what if she skipped a grade? Okay, it doesn't matter, it's just a fantasy, just go with it, just... yes, and he would keep her after school because she had forgotten how to square a quadratic... now, really Madeline, how could you forget that? And imagining her tight little breasts pressed up against those They Might Be Giants T-shirts and he would take off her glasses and... Madeline Hunter had acne and a bad bowl haircut and really, her pussy would be so tight because she was most definitely a virgin and...

Nope, it wasn't happening.... shut up shut up just keep with it... another girl then... another girl... keep looking on the internet... Oh, who is this girl, Bambi? Fine yes, Bambi a hot co-ed who "WANTS YOUR COCK" and he pictured shoving it in her, shoving it hard and hard and hardware store and that plum-shaped ass —

"Bert?"

He heard Joanne call down from upstairs in her half-awake voice, and he put his half chub back in his PJ pants and shuffled up to bed, defeated, even by internet porn.

At breakfast, Joanne gasped. She was futzing around with the laptop checking her email.

"Oh my God, Phil just died."

Phil? His mind searched for context.

Ah, yes. *Phil. Phil Goldstein.* Joanne had taken developmental psych classes from him back in the day, and they had become friends. Phil had been at their wedding. And about once a year or so they had Phil and his wife — he couldn't remember Phil's wife's name right now — over for dinner. He tried to not feel jealous of the man. This dead man.

And then Joanne gasped again, this time with even greater shock. "Have you been watching *porn*?" Her voice was shaking.

"No!" he said. "Of course, not!"

"Then why is this in my history?"

She turned the computer to face him:

TEEN SLUT WANTS YOU TO BEAT HER AND FUCK HER PUSSY

He was horrified. It had a girl in clear bondage with exposed vagina and definitely did not look like the sort of thing he, as a liberated male feminist, should be beating off to.

"Oh my God," he said, "what has Parker been looking at?"

Just right then, Parker was sleepily stepping in his sock feet toward the breakfast table, unaware of the onslaught he was about to receive.

Snow realized, as his son played patsy to his perversions, that he, as a good father, should feel at least a little bad about Parker losing his computer access for the next month. But he couldn't. Kids were too plugged in and addicted to technology anyway, and while his 9 year old son was currently innocent of the crime, Bert knew that Parker would spend enough time doing the crime in the next five years to be punished for it pre-committal.

Besides, Bert was absolutely going to kill himself this summer, and he didn't want others' memory of him besmirched with the truth. It would be better for everyone.

Chapter 19: Pick Up at a Funeral

The funeral was, like all funerals, long and boring. Goldstein had been Jewish, so it was a traditional Jewish ceremony, and Joanne was sobbing through the whole thing, so Mr. Snow was feeling extremely uncomfortable because not only was his wife a disaster, but he looked so callous as he couldn't even manage to look concerned.

Then he heard another high-pitched wail and a loud honk into a Kleenex.

It was *her*.

Hardware store girl. Sobbing like her cries could save the Titanic.

It was HER!

It was all he could do to not jump up in the middle of the service and rush over to her. He couldn't lose sight of her. She might disappear again. He didn't risk darting glances, though.

She might escape while his eyes were off of her. No more risks. He full on stared her down.

The moment the Rabbi moved off the stage Snow moved too, pushing to get through the crowd to her. He did his best to look as casual as he could, considering he'd mowed down about twelve people at a funeral to reach her.

"Hello! Hello! I met you at the hardware store!" he said.

What he saw in her eyes made him blush from pate to peter. She was thrilled to see him.

"You! I… I am so sorry I am terrible with names," she said, blowing her nose again.

They had caused a traffic jam, and he had left his wife sobbing three aisles over and as people pushed to get by him, he pushed into her.

That was the feel of her sweater — that was the scent of her hair — that was her touch.

"Bert Snow," he said. "And you are — ?"

"Dominique Colt. You know Dr. Goldstein?"

"*Know* him, oh yes. We are old friends, incredibly close friends and — "

"It's just so horrible," she said, her face wrecked.

God, he wished again, and so much harder, that he were Dr. Goldstein, that lucky bastard. People crying over his dead corpse.

Joanne was making her way towards him, hugging people as she walked in tears. He didn't have much time if he wanted to avoid his personal angel encountering his wife.

"Can we have coffee?" he asked, not trying to not seem too desperate. "I really want to talk to you. I really *need* to talk to you."

She did not think it unusual, some stranger she had

encountered months ago in a store suddenly pleading to see her, or she was grieving so deeply she didn't notice.

"Of course," she said. His phone was out, and she rattled off her digits. He inputted them and showed them back to her. The moment she nodded, and he knew for sure that he had her information at last, she turned to leave.

But he grabbed her quickly into a hug and held her. At last, he held her. He'd hold that moment just like that, just that feeling of finding her and holding her, forever.

Chapter 20:
"I want to be honest with you"

They'd agreed to meet at the Starbucks on Ventura and Laurel Grove. He'd arrived early. He didn't know whether to order coffee for her or wait for her to order her own coffee, and should he buy her coffee for her, or let her buy her own and why were they at Starbucks, anyway? Oh, he had suggested this Starbucks, far enough from his work and his home to make sure that he wouldn't be seen, because he did not want to be seen out on a Tuesday afternoon, drinking coffee with a woman he was going to proposition.

He'd decided that from the moment he saw her again. He didn't care that it was wrong, he didn't care whom it would hurt, he wanted to commit adultery and if she would give him the slightest opportunity, he would. He would beg, in fact. She could do whatever kinky things she wanted to him, if that's what she was into. In fact, he hoped she would. He tried to think of the worst possible things she could do to him, and he was fine with it. She could tie him up and pee in his mouth for all he cared, just as long as she also let him hold her for a while and whisper in her ear and tell her the truth that he didn't know what he had done with the past 46 years but he knew he didn't want to keep doing it.

So he came early, and he ordered the craziest drink he could think of. Usually he just drank tea, but today he went for something with vanilla mocha and caramel whipped and injected with enough espresso to fell an elephant.

And he waited. Until he saw her enter.

She wore little black jeans and no glasses and a yellow shirt with a big stripe on it that reminded him of Charlie Brown. Her skin shone and her hair was pulled back in a little headband. She spotted him and gave him a goofy smile. She had a little gap between her perfect white teeth, and he wondered how much of his tongue he could fit in that gap. She waved and waited in line while he tried to figure out whether he should wait and save the table or get up and greet her.

He waited.

She sat down, sipped her drink, and immediately asked about how he knew Dr. Goldstein. Though he hated bringing his wife into this, he had to tell her that his wife had been a student of Goldstein's, and he told a soft anecdote of how Goldstein would often come to dinner.

Tears immediately came to Dominique's eyes. "Do you know he had over 14,000 students in the course of his life?"

He didn't know that. As a teacher himself, he was amazed he'd taught so many and he prepared to tell her about what *he* did for a living, but she continued on with religious zeal.

Yes, she rattled off facts about Goldstein with a fever in her gold eyes. His parents escaped the Nazis in Germany, and he was a student of Frankl and Maslow, and he had been one of the first champions of this positive psychology of self-actualization and being.

"I remember in one class, he said, 'Nothing is more important than fully embracing your own life and the radical possibilities of self.' Isn't that beautiful? Isn't that just amazing?"

Snow nodded, hating that lucky dead bastard more and more with intensity.

"And to have him just end like *that*. To make it out of Nazi Germany and then to end so terribly."

"Well, it was his parents who escaped," Snow said, feeling it his duty to point that out. "He wasn't born yet."

"But to have come so far and done so much good and to just… die."

She cried again. He was confused.

"He was 71," he said gently.

"He had blood coming out of his eyes," she said. "He had blood coming out of his penis!"

"Jesus!" Snow said. "How do you know that?"

"Have you read anything about pancreatic cancer? Do you know how painful it is? Do you know how it turns your own blood against you? Do you know how incredibly he suffered?"

He was about to talk about what marvelous morphine derivatives he was sure they'd given him, but something in her look kept him silent.

"Well," he said, finally, "we all have to die."

She shrugged. "Maybe. One could always become a Vampire."

He almost choked. He knew better than to think she was

joking. That's what got him into trouble in the first place. Sincerity — that was this girl. Ridiculous and fucked up, sure, but sincere.

"Yes, and?" He must remember the rules of improvisation. He must radically accept all to keep it going.

"Yes, and…," she continued. "…I'm doing my Master's thesis on group-psychology and I'm studying the Vampires."

"Well, how fascinating!"

Yes, and! She was learning fascinating things about The Church of The Immortal Order. Did he know they actively recruited people in Hollywood and the Industry? Did he know that they believed in achieving immortality through technology? Did he know that —

And then she just stopped and looked into space for almost a full minute.

"Actually," she said. "I might just forget the whole thing. I might just leave school. I'm not sure. I really don't feel good about anything right now."

He stared at her, everything buzzing, alive and present and he knew what he had to say.

"Yes, and me neither," he said. "I don't feel good about anything right now. Except for one thing — you."

Her eyes met his.

Yes… and. Here they both were, now, in this moment in time together, so lucky.

"I want to be honest with you," Snow said. "I have a wife and a kid. And I love them both. But I would really like you to tie me up and beat me, and ruin my life."

And then, like a ripe avocado, he just opened up and scooped out his guts. He never talked as openly to anyone, ever, as he did right then. He supposed because she was training to be a psychologist, she was very good at just listening but he talked about everything from his busted dreams of being the next Steve Martin to his blaming his son for his internet porn. For a half hour he talked, barely taking a breath.

"Yes, and I love you," he finished. He hadn't even touched her hand, or her arm, or hugged her hello. He hadn't touched her at all.

She didn't respond, but kept looking at him with the same intent gaze.

He was worried. She was going to say, *"I'm flattered but,"* or *"I am in a serious relationship,"* both of which he had predicted would be true, but he didn't want her to say them. All he wanted her to say was, *"Yes. Yes and now."*

But instead she said, "What good will that do you? Ruining your life."

He didn't know how to respond.

"And what good will that do *me?*" she said. "I have a boyfriend, a gay lover and a fiancé, and honestly, I find sex rather tedious. So, as much as I want to help you and ruin your life if you want it ruined, I just don't think it would do either of us any good."

It was the worst thing she could possibly say, because it was true.

He looked down, nodding. And he was embarrassed, and spent, and sick of it.

"So what now, back to getting a therapist and talking and maybe I need some medication, or a more active lifestyle… or suicide? Yes, there's always that, right?"

"Are you suicidal, Bert?"

"Yes. YES. And the thought of you is the only thing that is keeping me going." He didn't mean to seem threatening. He didn't mean to hold it over her like that, but then here he was, doing it. " Yes, and I am asking of you — no I am begging of you — please, please help me."

He reached across the table and took her hand.

"Help me," he repeated.

She looked at him with determination. "Okay," she said. "I can help you. I know what I'll do."

He waited for her to gather her thoughts.

"I am going to develop a radical therapy to cure you."

Chapter 21:
Radical Therapy

The therapy would start with ten minutes of talking, then there would be forty-five minutes of radical experiential understanding split into a fifteen minute and thirty minute section. Between the two there would be a five-minute drink break.

She told him he must do whatever she requested without question.

She wanted him to experience his nakedness, his feelings of anxiety and feeling trapped in himself.

She told him he would be asked to remove his clothes and would experience bondage. He was not allowed to touch her or request to touch her.

She told him at some point in the bondage portion she would come in and he could request a drink, which she would bring for him to have through a straw.

She gave him a time and an address.

Bert drove his 1999, still working fine, Toyota Tercel down Reseda Blvd. with strip malls and traffic on one side and a thick sunshine sandwich of smog on the other. Her building was one of those peach-stucco eye-sores favored by non-forward thinking constructivists of the 1980's. There was a callbox with twenty names on it. He pressed the number she'd given him. Her voice came down through the speaker. He said his name, and she buzzed him in.

She came to the door wearing a long, brown sweater and leggings. In Los Angeles, 60 degrees is chilly. She brought him inside.

Her apartment was clean but cluttered, without art on the walls. It seemed like it was in the process of being moved into or out of. It was as non-descript an apartment as one could ask for. He supposed he could inspect the clutter, which seemed to be an assortment of papers, psychology text books, the various accoutrements they must give out in grad school these days.

But she hastened him through that room. She brought him into a room without a window. It was a bedroom, but the bedroom in a two-bedroom apartment the person paying $200 less rent would be assigned.

The room had horrible off-white plush carpet that was gray in spots. There were two chairs: A black office chair and a folding chair. And in the corner, a length of chain, the chain she'd bought in Al's Hardware, all those months ago.

He supposed the little metal folding chair was the appropriate place to be tortured, but she motioned him towards the other.

"You want to be as comfortable as possible, I think?" she

said. "Especially for the first one. I bought that chair just for you."

He made sounds of appreciation. Very kind of her.

She sat in the metal chair. She took out a legal pad and pen.

He thought about how cute she was, how serious right now, her forehead puckered, her pen poised. She looked at him expectantly.

"Do you want me to start talking?" he asked.

She started the timer in response.

"Oh, we're starting now?" he asked.

She nodded.

"What happens if we run over?"

"The clock is our boundary. We end on the bell."

"Very Pavlovian."

She gave him a 'good try' sort of smile.

"I wonder if I will start drooling for the milkshake."

"The milkshake?"

Oh shit, he'd let it slip what drink he was going to ask for. He wanted to surprise her in the moment. Make her scramble.

"I have been thinking a lot about what drink to ask for. I am thinking of a milkshake."

"I don't have a milkshake."

"Right."

"And I'm not going to leave you here bound in a chain to go get one."

"What *do* you have?"

"I have juice, cola, wine, beer, water, sparkling water, tonic water, and vitamin water."

"I guess you recommend I have water?"

"Well, I thought water would be the most natural choice. Or wine."

"Why natural?"

She hadn't written anything down on her pad of paper yet. "Is this really what you want to talk about?" she asked. "Five minutes have already passed."

"Oh, what else should I talk about?"

"Your suicidal thoughts."

"Oh. Yes. Well... I already have talked so much in our brief relationship and I would so much rather hear you talk. Talk about the lucky, lucky bastards who get to have sexual intercourse with you. Tell me what they did to earn that. Or tell me what I can do to earn it. I'll kill them all and eat their hearts for you. I'll give you cunnilingus on top of their corpses."

"Don't be weird."

"I don't think as a doctor you are supposed to say something is 'weird.'"

"I'm not a doctor."

"Okay, well, a shrink."

"I'm not a shrink."

"You're a student, though, and I'm just saying I've been to therapy before and I don't think you're supposed to say anything is weird. I could say I have sexual fantasies about monkey poop nuns fucking blood cum and you should just nod."

"Is that what your sexual fantasies are about?"

"Not at all."

"What do you fantasize about?"

"You."

Dominique looked at the timer. "What *about* me?

"The way you held that chain in the store, but then I think about how your hands are so small and what they would feel like on my face, and that your eyes are so warm and how I want them to just look at me and that your voice is so soft and how I would like to hear you sing."

"Those aren't very sexual thoughts."

"Is that a criticism?"

"Not at all. But you said 'sexual fantasies.'"

"No, *you* said, 'What do you fantasize about?' You didn't specify sexual."

"Well then, what do you fantasize about *sexually*?"

DING.

He could tell she was upset. That this wasn't going at all like she had hoped. Her paper had scribbles of barely legible writing, but he had thrown her.

He hadn't meant to. He hadn't meant to go all Ionesco play on her. She was obviously a serious student working on a serious thesis and maybe —

Her hands were suddenly on him.

She was unbuttoning his shirt. Her head came just beneath his, her small head with brown hair he could tell she straightened, and he could see she couldn't quite part her hair properly.

He breathed her in.

He reached his hands up and held hers in his. Her hands were so soft. Her nails were unpainted and trimmed very short.

"You don't touch me," she reminded him, softly.

He moved his hands away and back at his side.

His shirt was unbuttoned. He was aware of just how middle-aged he was. He tried to keep in pretty good shape, but his belly protruded. He had hair in patches on his chest and belly. He hadn't thought of this part, of just being this lump of flesh and hair and whatever else, but he didn't feel ashamed.

"Your hands feel nice," he said.

"Maybe I should gag you first," she chided.

"Am I not supposed to talk?"

"This is supposed to be the ceremonial stripping away of you to your basic essence," she said, having trouble with his belt. "I am trying to get you to feel your human condition-ness, your animal-ness."

"Animal-ness?" he offered, her face at his crotch, it was too easy. He didn't make a lewd movement, the word alone felt like an affront enough.

She got the belt open, undid his zipper without ceremony. She pulled down his pants.

He was wearing black briefs. He'd purchased them particularly for this occasion. She pulled them down, exposing his penis, which was at a half-salute, like a little bald man's head winking a good eye into the sunlight to see if it was warm enough to come out.

"Step out of them, please." His briefs were around his ankles and he obliged. He was smiling. He was having a nice time, so far. He did feel bad that she seemed to be stressed about it.

"Sit down," she ordered, in a voice that was more of a bark than he had heard from her before.

He sat, feeling the faux leather of the chair sticking to his flesh. He heard the clank of the chain. He felt suddenly alarmed. She hadn't quite coiled it in a way she could lift so she was humphing and hefting it.

"You need help?" he asked.

She shot him a look that kept him seated. Breathing heavily, she held half the chain.

"Did you ever use this on anyone else?" he asked.

"I am not at liberty to disclose," she said, as if that were true.

"I just want to be sure that it has been sanitized."

"Will you *shut... up?*"

"Are you supposed to tell people to shut up? Isn't the whole point of therapy to talk?"

She dropped the chain with a thwack and went back to the desk, grabbing a long red piece of cloth.

Oh. The gag.

She wrapped the gag around his mouth. It wasn't very tight. He opened his mouth to tell her so and it fell off.

"I think it would work better if you put it inside my mouth," he said.

"Huh?"

"Usually with a gag it should go inside the mouth, I think."

"How is that a gag, then? Your mouth is open."

"Yes, but it makes it difficult to… it actually gags you, that's why it's called a gag."

"Oh. Okay."

"Try it." He opened his mouth, and she pushed the cloth inside and tied it around his head.

"uch- eer" ("much better"), he said.

He did his best to show her a smile.

She pulled the chain off the ground again. She laced one end around him.

It was cold. It was already boring into his skin a bit, even though it wasn't tight. His penis had decided to make a full retreat back into his body. Not warm at all.

She pulled the chain through the chair arms, then around his arms and torso, winding it around twice. She looped it under the chair and pulled it around his legs. Then she left it.

It wasn't the most professional job. It wouldn't take too much effort to get out of it. She hadn't even locked it. He would have pointed this out but for the gag.

Oh well, he was playing along and he didn't want to be

chained all that tight anyway, but if the point was to make him feel the anxiety —

She put the blindfold on. It was one of those airplane eye masks. He almost laughed, but of course, the gag. And then it was darker.

Then he heard the timer go on and the door shut.

At first he tried to focus on how softly he was trapped. The ease it would be to get out of the mask. The simplicity in which he could struggle against the chain, how cold the chain was, how it was already irritating his skin. Then he tried to focus on what she had said he *should* focus on: Being trapped and anxious, and maybe in a way it was a good analogy. He really *was* only softly trapped in his life, as well. Couldn't he off himself at any time if he really wanted to?

And then he started to think about her, how she was actually trying to help him, how weird this idea was that she had for therapy, how it already seemed more effective than his previous encounters with therapists, and how he was excited about their sessions, and how he would try to be a better subject.

What drink should he ask for? She obviously wanted him to ask for water, so he would ask for water. But did she care if it was regular, sparkling or vitamin?

He would not struggle against these chains. Personally, he thought she had not gone far enough, first of all, an hour was far too short of an amount of time, she obviously did not know what she was doing with the chains and gags and all that. Had he asked her if she was actually *into* BDSM? It didn't seem like it. He was certain people in that community would have a better idea of what they were doing. Maybe she was, as she had said, just trying her best to find a more effective means of therapy. That was admirable…

Could he tell his wife about this therapy? She'd be happy he was going back to therapy, but she probably wouldn't be too happy that he was doing experimental therapy with an unlicensed beauty whom he'd met in a hardware store. What was that Martin Amis thing about smoking?

How much time had passed?

Surely, it must be about to end now. He really was very uncomfortable. VERY uncomfortable. His foot was asleep. The chain was boring into his chest, and it had caught a couple of his chest hairs and was pulling them. He tried to scooch in the seat, but the pleather stuck to his skin. Also, he thought the chain would give more when he moved, but he actually discovered, as he moved it seemed to get tighter.

Tighter. Could he really get out of it, if he tried?

He was going to be a good patient. But as a good patient, shouldn't he help her test her practice? Then again, he didn't really want to be her patient, he really wanted her to — well, to just come back. This was too long already.

He was squirming now. Surely she would walk in at any minute now. She wouldn't have tricked him, she wouldn't just leave him here. Unless she changed her mind and was going to go out and get the milkshake. What if she got hit by a car? What if... of course, he could get out. It was easy. The chain wasn't even locked. He squirmed against it, but it certainly didn't feel like it was getting any looser. In fact, it was boring into him more now, it was really cutting off his circulation... it was too tight... he was going to need to get something amputated. Oh that would be great, just great to have one less limb to show him just how lucky he'd been this whole time with his disgusting self-pity, his disgusting tendency to feel so —

The gag was hurting his mouth. His mouth was dry. How

long had it been? It had to have been fifteen minutes at this point. It was ridiculous. How could it still be happening? How could he still be here? Oh, he was starting to panic now. Maybe she would leave him here to die. Maybe she would kill him, maybe… God, how much time was *left*?

He heard the distant patter of her footsteps. The timer still hadn't dinged. He could hear her outside, shuffling her feet. She was waiting for it. She was waiting for it. She would never leave him here. She was to be trusted, he trusted her, with his life —

DING.

The door opened. He tried to catch his breath, look calm, like the best test subject ever. She removed the gag, and he tried to suck saliva back into his mouth. Her hands seemed impossibly soft now.

"What would you like to drink?" she asked.

"A milkshake."

"I don't have a milkshake."

"What do you have?"

"I already told you."

"I'll have a vitamin water."

"Okay."

She stepped outside of the room.

He was crying.

That was weird. He was crying.

She put a straw in his mouth. What came through the straw seemed so impossibly sweet. He drank it all.

"What brand of water is that?"

"Shhh," she said.

The bell dinged again.

"I am putting the gag back on."

"That was five minutes? That didn't seem like five minutes."

"It was five minutes, now the gag goes back on."

"The chain is really hurting me — a lot. It's incredibly, terribly painful — "

But the gag was back on his mouth.

"Think about this, now, for the rest of the time. It'll be more time than it was before. Think about this. It's a Jean-Paul Sartre quote: 'Life begins on the other side of despair.'"

And then he heard the door close.

He thought about his whole life. How he had given up pursuing what he'd wanted once. Why? Because it seemed foolish and impossible, but now, everything seemed that way. And what could he do now, now that he knew he was nothing and had nothing to lose?

He was surprised when the timer went off because time could not have passed that quickly. But there it was, already over.

He heard her come back. She undid the chain. She was clumsy with it, and he was sure he had some bruising.

And then the best part. Her hands went to the spots that had hurt the most, and they softly kneaded into them. He felt as if something beneath his skin was bursting into life beneath her touch, on his legs, his torso.

And then the gag came off. He didn't say anything yet, though.

And then the eye mask.

When he looked and saw her face he thought it was quite possibly the most brilliant thing he had ever seen. He had thought her eyes were gold. They were not. They were gray. Dove gray. How could he have mistaken something like that? And she had little freckles on her face. And her nose was slightly crooked. And —

"Get dressed, now. And then leave. "

She turned and walked out and closed the door.

He put his clothes on. And when he walked outside the room, the front door was wide open, and she was no longer there.

Chapter 22:
How This Would
Look in a Movie

Madeline is supposed to pick up Dieter at 4:45 a.m. so he could make his flight.

She set the alarm on her phone, but forgot to save it. Thus, when she awakens at 7:18 a.m., past when his flight to Germany would be long in the sky, she is sure she would never feel more like shit. She is very wrong.

Why hasn't he called? She calls him, letting him know she is on her way, she is sorry, she is a shitty friend. She talks as she drives, she curses traffic, figuring she will double park rather than battle for street parking, but as she pulls up she sees two cop cars.

And his front door is wide open.

She knows this must be a dream as she walks toward the

two cops and the open door because the air around her has this thickness and she can hear her heart, her legs threatening to buckle, and she thinks that if she can just lay down on the grass and close her eyes she will wake up back in her bed to her phone alarm buzzing.

But instead, conversation follows — her mouth opens and says, "Blah blah blah" and the cops talk back through layers of water and sand.

Apparently, she has just missed the paramedic.

Apparently, the landlord had let himself in when Dieter's alarm wouldn't stop going off. Two hours, it had buzzed.

Apparently, Dieter is dead.

Apparently, they couldn't say now for sure, but it looks like a suicide.

Mads stands there, thinking about how this would look in a movie. She is thinking about what she would direct herself to do and what the appropriate response would be.

She should wail. Cry. Beat her breasts. But she doesn't cry in front of people. Not now, even. She couldn't. She is directing herself to cry – ready, action! – but there is nothing but the sounds of a normal, shitty street in L.A. all around her, with phony people — phony cops — were these real cops or actors? They could be both, she supposes. Actor cops. Why not? Phony landlord? Would she cast *this* guy as the landlord? No. Fire him. She could find a better landlord "type."

Wait. She needed to take Dieter to the airport. He had probably already missed his plane but —

Her knees buckle. She's half on the concrete, half on grass covered in dogshit.

No one comes over to help her, though one of the cops makes a motion to do so. He comes close and she asks, "Was he wearing the cross?"

The cop asks her to repeat the question, which she does, and then elaborates about it being "protection." At which point they peg her as a religious nut and no, they don't remember a cross, not that cop, nor the other, nor the landlord, and the fucking paramedics are gone already. She doesn't know why she keeps harping on it, but of course she would know as soon as her brain comes back to her.

But for now, she starts screaming about it, screaming like a director throwing a diva-fit, screaming like a director who'd throw tepid coffee in the face of a P.A., a King of The Fucking World screaming, *"Was he or was he not wearing the FUCKING CROSS?"*

The people cast as the cops do not taze her or take her downtown and book her for disorderly conduct and lack of proper respect for armed officers. Because she is a young and attractive-ish white girl they do not shoot her down for being threatening, even though she lunges at them.

No, she is not threatening. She is a woman.

And they try not to laugh.

But she doesn't cry in front of anyone.

There would be a time later to establish all of the details. Apparently, an overdose on a weird prescription he'd been taking. Apparently, it was intentional, and apparently whatever his sentimental attachment to the cross, it is nowhere to be found, neither in his apartment nor on his body.

And while this would be, to the county of Los Angeles, death by suicide, Madeline knows, like she knows nothing else in this world, that he has been murdered.

She feels a pure white-hot hatred stronger than she has ever felt. More than she hated *Tranformers 29*, posers, bigots and Hitler. She fucking hated the fucking Vampires with a *feel the dark side of the Force* type of hatred that was so strong in her, it demanded vengeance.

And she would have it.

There is no relief but in one thought:

She is going to stake Vince Vaughn.

Chapter 23:
Jesus Climax

Frau Gerta Künstwerk is a German pancake sleeping on Mads' studio apartment floor. Gerta, with her ash blonde hair and marble blue eyes, looks like the fat and beaten grown-up version of the littlest Von-Trapp from "The Sound of Music." She doesn't mind having only a sleeping bag and being something Mads keeps stepping over, probably because she is consistently near-blackout drunk and sobbing, "Why my boy kill himself? Why?" in a thick German accent.

Frau Künstwerk is having his ashes sent back to Germany so she can scatter them there, and have a service for his family there, but there is a memorial service at the crematorium, as well. Julian is there, and people from USC, a few drunk and crying bears from caves past, and a couple of shifty looking Flashy Talent people. It is a sad-as-fuck showing.

Gerta grabs Madeline in an embrace as she holds the urn,

like the two of them were group-hugging Dieter. As Madeline holds the sobbing woman who has yet-to-get-drunk because it is 11:00 in the afternoon and she is trying to be sober-ish for the memorial, Gerta whispers, "He had said he had embraced God. He said he had found Christ. Was he just lying to me?"

And then Madeline tells her, also in a whisper, that she doesn't believe Dieter killed himself, and she is going to find the ones who did this to him and bring them to justice. Mads tells her just like she would tell her if it were a revenge movie, and Gerta gets the fire back in her eyes and nods.

Dieter *couldn't* have killed himself because he had just found such meaning and purpose in a new religion that meant so much to him.

Gerta becomes excited. Could they go to this church? Could she meet the people who had meant so much to him?

So Madeline calls John Lee — John Lee who had not heard, John Lee who, upon hearing the news, wails and cries tears she has not been able to cry. And whereas Madeline expects some bullshit from John Lee about how Dieter had thrown away God's greatest gift, instead, Lee immediately blames the Vampires, as well. And they need to make more people aware of their danger.

She doesn't tell him she is gonna stake their most famous celebrity member — figures it's best for him not to know. Plausible deniability and all.

And Lee insists on a proper service for his "Brother in Christ."

There is now a memorial for Dieter at the Cross-Fire church, which is a recreation hall on the outskirts of the CSUN campus. Madeline is secretly worried she might burst into flame going into any religious room or service, but to her surprise, she enters unscathed.

There is a froggy-faced woman with a bad page-boy haircut who hugs both her and Gerta as they enter, and gives them a little piece of paper with Dieter's face photocopied on to it. And there's a slew of dumb-as-rocks looking college kids. And a man who looks like a loser, a completely unscary version of Slender Man. And a lady with fried blonde hair who is so fat, she actually waddles. What a congregation! Frau Künstwerk must be mortified. But on the contrary, she seems to be taking great comfort in these creatures who bleat and moo about eternal rewards and the triumph of Christ.

And then there is this makeshift band of cute college boys and girls who play some soft rock song they've probably written themselves: *"Jesus, how you make me feel,"* and Mads is thinking how changing the intonation could make it blasphemous, or dirty, or both. But then John Lee starts talking, and it starts to take great effort for Madeline to be able to get her thoughts in to amuse herself because his voice makes something in her pay attention (*Stop! Notice! Stop!*).

"The death of Dieter," John Lee says, "is the least interesting thing that happened to Dieter. Death and pain are a guarantee of this world — the mortification of the flesh. No, the most interesting thing about Dieter…

(*oh do tell, do tell, you fucker who barely knew him*)

"…is that he turned to Christ. That he turned away from sin, that he opened his heart to Jesus, who reclaimed his soul, which he had sold for the false promise of immortality, and instead he was given true immortality — in Christ!"

Madeline feels like she might puke right now, but that she has to be strong for Dieter's German mom, who is a sniveling wreck of "Ja! Ja! Ja! Dieter!" She can see, in Dieter's mom, the same pudding of a face, the same little eyes. It's like looking at the middle-aged female version of her dead friend.

Her dead friend. They probably pried his mouth open and forced the pills down his throat. It must have hurt him. Did they give him something to wash it down? Or did they just force it down him while he cried out in pain?

"When Jesus had the nails pierced through him," Lee exhorts, "and was crucified, there was great weeping and gnashing of teeth. But now, we celebrate. We celebrate His suffering because He has shown us how to triumph over suffering, the ultimate triumph over any violent death, no matter how horrible. For He gives us purpose! Meaning!"

(*What? What? STOP NOTICE WHAT?*)

"Madeline Hunter," John Lee says, "I can see the spirit of Christ is upon you, descending like a dove. Madeline Hunter, will you open your heart to Jesus?"

(*Oh God — They are all looking at me — these people — Froggy face and SlenderloserMan and Friedblondefatlady and Dieter's mom, too*).

Yes, and she can feel it.

She can.

(*fucking feel it-They love me*) —

They fucking love her —

But more than that, there is this other thing

(*Fuck no*)

This feeling coming from inside her and

She loves them —

(I love *them*)

She fucking *loves* them!

Her heart starts expanding. She feels like the Grinch in the story when he sees the Whos singing — it's thumping and expanding and her eyes feel all watery and then it's like her insides start shining, everything starts shining, reflecting back everyone else's shining and everyone and

(*Everything is so fucking beautiful so fucking perfect — so fucking real —*

Life is real and earnest

Life is wild and good

Life is true

Life is spirit

Life is light that is shining out of everyone and everything brimming)

And no wonder she can't see it all the time —

(*It is too fucking much — it is too fucking real*)

And she can't stop thinking and saying fucking because otherwise it's just

(*God god god god god Jesus God Jesus God*

Fuck fuck fuck)

Her soul is having an orgasm and she is about to cum right out the top of her head and into the universe but instead it is coming out of her eyes and she is sobbing weeping crying and she is holding and hugging people she has felt nothing but contempt for nothing but as if they were trash these people — these people are holding her as she sobs on their shoulders.

And their faces are the faces of God.

(*Jesus*

Jesus

This is Jesus).

And now this person — Froggy face — Froggy face is

Jesus' face, too. And Slenderloserman — he is Jesus, too. And John Lee — who is holding her now — of course, they all are — Jesus is all of them and her, her too.

The Kingdom of God is within you. The Kingdom of Heaven is among you.

"Madeline Hunter," John Lee says, "will you be saved?"

Her whole being rocking in climax with a moan as she utters…

"Yes!"

And her heart lets go with a rush she cannot stop as she comes to Jesus.

Chapter 24: The Morning After

Madeline is stuck in crappy LAX traffic, taking Frau Künstwerk to the airport. Gerta is sober and while still crying, she seems more at peace. Madeline talks in her head, trying to make sense of what happened.

(*What was it I needed? It was that thought — that thought that I was so alone, that I was so selfish, that I never had a real friend but Dieter and he's dead and gone and there's nothing now but nothing and I called for help and they saw my need and told me I was never alone — but — nevermind anymore. Everyone is entitled to a group-think brainwash every once in a while.*)

She looks out the window.

She drops Frau Künstwerk off at the airport with a quick hug and then has to move along because of traffic — "No parking, No waiting," as the sign says — and that is the end of that.

So then it's just her again. Alone. Driving the 405 North. She thinks back on it.

(Did I really say "Yes!"? "Saved"? What bullshit.)

And she vows to never think on it again.

Chapter 25: Dominique Loses It

With $65,000 dollars in student loan debt, Dominique received word that she had been put on academic probation. She had not been to classes in a month, had not met with the new chair to whom she'd been re-assigned, and was in danger of failing all of her classes and being kicked out of her program.

Later that day, Dominique lost her gay lover, her boyfriend and her fiancé to someone else. It went something like this:

It started with Jim asking her to join in on another three-some, which she did, because she didn't want him to stay mad at her. This was the opposite of fun because this third, a twinkie named Hal, was only pretending to be straight to play to Jim's straight-guy fetish and within five seconds, he was all over Jim and they both left her out entirely. Naked and feeling bored, she wandered away from the two of them to the record player where Janis Joplin was singing about pieces of her heart.

Neither Jim nor Hal called her back over.

Jim was on all fours and Hal was ramming him to the beat the band.

Meanwhile, Dominique got dressed.

"Hey, I'm gonna go ahead and go," she called over to them.

No one looked up to even say, *"Goodbye."*

As she walked down the street to her car, her phone buzzed. It was her virile young boyfriend, Dave.

"Hi!" she said, excited to hear his voice.

"Hey," he said. There was something wrong. "Um, I'm just gonna come out and say this, but uh, I think uh, well, I'm seeing someone else."

"Oh?" she said.

"So, I'll see you around sometime or something, okay?"

"Okay."

And just that fast, she'd lost her boyfriend. So knowing this was a day to stay in the apartment, not answer the phone, Dominique locked the door behind her. Within ten minutes there was a knock.

She didn't answer it.

But then a key turned in the lock. Was it Georgia, her studious roommate and possible maid of honor back from the library?

"Hello? Dominique?" a tentative voice called out as the door opened. No, it was Felix. That's right. Felix, her betrothed, back from some time apart, Felix, being her fiancé, had a key.

Oh God.

"Hi Felix, in here," she said from the bedroom.

He entered, with his mop of curly hair, his doughy boy face sporting a practiced smile. "Hi," he said. "How are you?"

How was she?

"Okay," she said.

He was sure to have a monologue now. And he didn't disappoint. He sat on her bed.

"The past year has been such an incredible growth experience for me. I feel you are so smart and such a great student. You will be the most brilliant doctor-psychologist out there, the top of the field. You will be a famous doctor, and everyone will know about you."

She didn't mention the academic probation. She did mention the lovely engagement gift Georgia had purchased for them, a fine-crafted artisan brick for their new apartment or home.

He inspected it, found it kitschy and horrible.

"Well, we should probably register some place to make sure we get gifts we like," Dominique suggested as there were many family members already wanting to purchase things for this undated wedding.

At which point Felix said, "About the wedding… I think maybe we should hold off on thinking about it just yet, because you know. Well, I wanted to talk to you. You know, with your whole thing about the three-way…"

"My whole thing?"

"Yes. That was your idea. You wanted to make Jim feel better."

"No, I am pretty sure that was *your* idea."

"It was definitely *your* idea, no doubt about it," he said. "But listen, all this is besides the point because all I am saying now is I think I'm done with my experimenting."

Dominique breathed a sigh of relief. Oh, Felix! Back to normalcy! To being a normal couple. "Good," she said. "Me, too."

Felix smiled. "I think we should do a three-way with Connie; she works at Green Grocer, you'll really like her."

"Wait, you just said you were done with experimenting."

"With guys. But I think if we tried it with another *girl*, I think it would really make it work for me. You had what you wanted with the three-way with two guys, I think I should get what I want with the three-way with two girls. Because if we're gonna get married, we need to make sure that we always treat each other fairly."

Dominique sat across a table at Chipotle with Felix and Connie. Connie was a little punk with pink hair and a nose ring. She looked about nineteen. Connie didn't giggle or anything, but she kept posting on her phone the whole time, which was one of Dominique's pet peeves. Felix was oblivious, as he was giving a monologue about cryogenics and the Singularity.

"And when living to be 200, 300 years old becomes commonplace, ten years for interplanetary travel will seem like less of a big deal."

Connie looked up. "Huh?"

"Which is why I think we need to actively start thinking about colonizing other planets now."

"Right, totally," Connie said.

"Those are the sorts of things we think about," Felix said, including Dominique now, in this monologue. Dominique gave a quick nod.

"But Dominique and I don't think about things in bourgeois sort of ways. We're engaged and all, but we have an open relationship."

This was the first Dominique had heard it described like that. An open relationship. Was it *that*?

Connie still seemed bored. "Well, cool," she said without feeling. "Cool for you guys."

"So," Felix said, and gave her an expectant look. "Maybe Dominique can explain better."

And that's when Dominique realized Felix hadn't brought up the three-way to Connie, that this was supposed to be *her* job. Frankly, she was already having a sinking sort of feeling that she hated her fiancé. This would not bode well for the marriage.

Dominique was silent.

"Tell her," Felix prodded.

"I practice radical therapy," Dominique said.

That got Connie's attention. "Really? What do you do?"

"It involves a kind of existential process involving enacting a Foucault-type role play of power."

"Huh. Is Foucault a foreign filmmaker?"

"No, he's a philosopher. Foucault talked a lot about power and authority in roles and how these roles are enacted. The therapy I am developing is about doctor and patient type of enactments, as well as using some type of bondage."

At this point, Connie would be willing to sleep with her, regardless of her orientation. Felix knew it, Dominique knew it, and if Connie didn't know it, it wouldn't take a feather to knock her into it. But Dominique stopped talking and gave her best to the burrito she had in front of her.

Felix tried to pick up where she left off.

"I think actually, she developed some of her practices in this three-some we were — "

"No, no, no," Dominique said, mouth full.

"No?" he asked.

"No. That was all about a climax, and my procedure is all about an apocalypse."

Connie's mouth was slightly open. "Like, a Zombie Apocalypse?"

"Apocalypse," Dominique said, "as in… revelation. Awakening."

Connie looked down at her burrito with a troubled expression. "I'd be into that," she said.

"Oh — and maybe I could assist?" asked Felix.

"I don't have assistants, Felix, sorry." She turned to her potential subject. "Do you suffer from depression, anxiety, feelings of worthlessness, angst, or suicidal tendencies?"

"I think depression is the scar of humanistic castration by capitalism — " Felix began. This was his hook to start another rant.

But Dominique cut him off, ignoring him. "If you're seriously interested, Connie, get my number from Felix. I am still in the research phase and if you were willing, I'd take you on as a subject."

"Really?"

"Well, it's worth exploring. Let's talk."

Felix was so far into denial that he refused to address how Dominique had just cock-blocked him. They went back to her place, Felix moved in to kiss her, and Dominique accepted. She was bored, not interested, but she supposed commitment meant sometimes you did things you were bored and not interested in.

"Hey," Felix said, "it was interesting, and I think Connie will go for it, but why did you lie to Connie about that therapy stuff?"

"I wasn't lying. I've started doing a new type of therapy."

"Well," Felix said, "if that's true, that's really not okay."

"Why not?"

"Because first of all, you don't have a degree or a license, so you shouldn't be practicing as a therapist. I'm sure if I mentioned that to my therapist, she'd report you."

"Since when do you have a therapist?" It was the first time Dominique actually felt Felix was cheating on her.

"I don't know, a few months I guess."

"You didn't tell me that."

"Well, yeah, I guess I've just been feeling kinda stuck, and don't take this the wrong way, but I'm not sure I really want to marry you. So I thought I should talk to a therapist and get my mind sorted out."

Dominique felt a flash of fire. Everything burning, all that she knew. Past, present and future.

She took the ring off her finger and handed it to him.

It might have been at that moment that all the good sense Dominique possessed decided to curdle and harden. And she knew that she hated herself with a hatred so deep and strong that she felt she could tear her own face off and flush it down the toilet.

And then they had sex.

And she didn't see him again until the day she murdered him.

What acceptable motive was there for such a thing?

There was none. Zero.

Zilch.

But the defense made all sorts of claims:

First, that she had nothing to do with it. It was the

Vampires. She was investigating them, and because she knew too much, they were making an example of her by killing the men she loved.

Then they claimed it was an accident, that she was developing some radical sexual therapy and it went too far.

Then it was temporary insanity. She had been kicked out of school and stressed, depressed, and then was visited by Jim and Felix whom she claimed raped her and sodomized her… and she snapped.

But the prosecution had plenty of witnesses — Connie, Dave, Georgia, who all painted different sides of this very disturbed woman. The record showed that Dominique Colt had acted with premeditation. She had waited until her roommate was gone to a week-long conference in Boston and placed a call to both Jim and Felix. Then she had chained up the two boys, gagged them and then slowly and deliberately killed them.

Two boys were dead.

And there might be a third.

There was hair, skin and semen from a third man.

This was the Mystery Man.

If he were killed, where was the body? And if he was alive, why was he not coming forward?

Chapter 26:
Bertie's Sunny Day
of Reckoning

"I'm not happy, Bert."

He and Joanne were out walking on a Saturday afternoon, and he was just thinking how much better he'd been feeling.

"Since Phil died, I've been thinking a lot, and I have realized that I need to reconsider a lot of things in my life. And that includes you. Bert, I don't love you anymore."

If she had started rolling around on the ground and speaking in tongues he could not have been more surprised.

"And I don't think I have for years," she added.

He couldn't help it. He started in with an attack. How could she say something like that to him?! Didn't she know all he had done for her? All he had suffered for her? All he could think was that she must not — she could not, absolutely not

— leave him. He was willing to die before letting her go! To die!

But as he started spewing his rage, and she spewed it right back, it was clear that they were fighting over how many kicks they could get at a dead horse, so dead it was just a bag of bones.

Chapter 27:
Mads' Bluff

She has to place the right kind of trap. If she can scare them, make them think she knows more than she does... How did they do it? How can she prove it? If only she could *know* what happened.

What if Mads had been in Dieter's closet, that night he died? What if she had recorded everything that happened there that night?

Who is to say she hadn't?

She goes to The Order's official website. Just being on that site was probably infecting her poor laptop with a million Vampire viruses in a trail of little Vampire cookies. There is, of course, something stupid and cryptic written onscreen:

You have knocked.

She clicks on it.

Come in.

A chat room.

What do you need to know?

That is a good question. What does she need to know? She should start with something BS.

She types:

-So, you guys just wanna take people and drink their blood or what?-

The reply comes quickly:

-Many might think that, but it is a shallow interpretation. Pain is part of a Vampire's pleasure. We recognize that we bring pain to others, and that it feeds us. We recognize that feeding is pleasure. We do not condone hurting for its own sake, only for the purpose of feeding. There is, for those who willingly submit to be our food source, a reported sense of deep pleasure in satisfying a Vampire, and for many, the desire to become one of us. As you should be aware, being bitten or having your blood drank does not mean one becomes a Vampire. Rather it is a process that is far more complex and involves a ritualistic acceptance. There are no Vampires but the ones we have created. Any so-called vampire who lays claim to being a vampire without being inducted is a liar and a regular human. Does that answer your question?-

Well, Jesus, she didn't need a fucking novel.

-I am interested in joining the C class- she types.

-That is by invitation only-

-I have been invited-

-Then why are you asking?-

-I am testing you.-

-It is not wise to test Vampires-

Madeline takes a deep breath and types with fury:

-Look nube, George Clooney is going to star in the feature that I'm writing and directing. And I've been invited, all right? So don't you fucking test me-

The reply:
-Perhaps we should meet-
-I don't want to meet you. *I want to meet a level 5 C class or nothing-*
-Where and when can you meet?-

The Bar on Ventura and Cahuenga was one of those vintage bars with the red textured wallpaper and music that wasn't too loud. Madeline is smacking her gum, which she is chewing piece after piece in a nervous habit she picked up instead of smoking back in the high school days of standardized testing.

The second he enters she knows this is the one they sent to her. He is probably some sort of talent agent. He looks tired, like maybe he'd been called out of bed.

"Talent agent?" Madeline says. "That's who they send to me? I'm directing a movie with George Clooney."

"I am not a talent agent, I am a casting director," he says. "And I happen to know everyone who has hired George Clooney in the past year, and you are not one of them." But he gives her his hand. "My name is Rick Westing, and I am a member of The Order. I will say you have an aura of bravado that is appealing."

"Yeah," she says. "Tell me about it."

"Well, I can tell that you have experienced tragedy recently and — "

"It's just an expression, I really am *not* interested in hearing about your psychic abilities."

He flashes her a smile with slight fang. "What is your name?"

"Dominique Colt," she tells him.

"Ha, ha," he says. "Very funny. Why are you unwilling to reveal your name?"

"Maybe you guys scare me," she says. "I don't know." She pops more gum into her mouth.

"Okay, 'Dominique Colt,'" he says with a grin. "Let me tell you this, if you really are part of the Hollywood industry, and want to be more than you are, there is nothing better than joining The Order for your career. The Church of the Immortal Order is very serious about amassing success in this world because it helps draw victims to it."

"Victims?"

"Right now we just suck people's energy. It is important not to suck people's blood until you have gone through the transformation into full Vampire, which has only happened to our leader at this point. And then, only on a consensual basis. It is important to us to maintain the laws of our society to forgo persecution."

"Okay...."

Then Westing proceeds to describe what sounds like a very elaborate pyramid scheme, where pretty much 10% of one's income before taxes immediately goes to the order, and then one's devotion is measured by how much one begins to give to Dr. Whaley, or "Dr. Dracula," as they like to call him, for surgeries. But gifts and devotion are measured not only by money, but also in trades and favors. Dr. Whaley's staff of interns, maids, personal assistants, and nurses are almost entirely nubes.

"But *you* won't stay a nube for long, I can tell," Westing assures her. "You can probably be a Level 2 within a few months. The ranks are easy to ascend through Level 3, but every Level is exponentially harder, so the higher one reaches, the harder it is to rise." Westing then spends some time explaining exponents to Mads, incorrectly.

Stage 5, where he was, is where they learn to suck people's energy at will.

"For example, how do you feel right now?" Westing asks.

Mads shrugs.

"Well, I have been steadily draining your energy for the last twenty minutes and feeding off it. You should feel tired, depressed and hopeless."

If that were the case, fucking Vampires had been feeding on her, and most of the general population, for years.

"I however," he said, "have been eating your light and feel energized, excited, and if I asked you to go with me to the bathroom right now, you'd let me fuck you."

"Uh, no thanks," she said.

"Wow, you are very powerful to resist me," Westing said. "But I assure you there are Vampires you could not resist."

"How do you handle resistance within The Order?"

"We have no resistance in The Order."

"What happens if you get up the ranks and you decide to leave?"

"It is an eternal commitment."

"But what if… let's just say… I don't know… what if I am this assistant over at Flashy Talent and I am all into it and then, suddenly, I'm not? If I tried to leave then would I end up, like, dead? Apparent suicide?"

Westing looks decidedly worried.

"Listen," she says, putting on her best hustler. "I don't want to bust any Vampire balls or anything. I just want to meet Vince Vaughn. I want him to be in my movie. That's all. Do you think you could arrange that for me?"

He certainly does not.

"How high up are you, again?" she asks.

"You don't just start in The Order and get to meet one of our highest level officiates… unless, of course… you want be a Juice Box." He slides a hand over towards her, which she smacks down on, hard enough to make her own hand sting and make him yelp.

"Listen, you piece of shit agent," Madeline says, smacking her gum, her voice calm, collected, like she is explaining how some simple mathematical operation works. "Stop fucking around and trying to pick up on me. I've got some shit on you guys that, when it settles, will make that Dominique Colt case look like fairy dust in comparison. I've got proof. I've got it ready to mail out to all the big papers that hate your fucking Twilight-pansy asses and they are just waiting for the fucking call. Do you hear me? I've got fucking proof that you vamps are responsible for MURDER. So get your ass in gear and get me Vince Vaughn."

She drops her gum in his drink and walks out.

She feels like a bad ass until she gets to her car and has to check the back seat four times and then gets in fast and locks the door and drives away as quickly as she can. Now she is glad she had never trusted herself to have a pet, because she would have to leave that pet forever because she is never going home again.

She is scared shitless.

There is really only one person she can turn to for help.

Chapter 28:
The Holy Family

"Madeline!" John Lee says, as if her waking him up at 1:30 am was a treat for him.

"You haven't been returning my calls!"

"Well, that's because you call me every fucking day and spout some Bible verse and it's fucking annoying."

"Well, after your conversion process at the church — "

"I didn't convert, okay? I didn't convert. So don't say that. I had an experience, but it was just grief and my being overwhelmed and thank you, it was a great experience, but it doesn't mean I accept Jesus into my heart."

"But you already said you did. In front of the congregation."

"Okay, whatever, I did. Look, that's not why I'm calling."

"Why *are* you calling?"

"I'd really like to sleep on your couch. I'm worried if I go home it will be crawling with Vampires."

"Oh?"

"Yeah, they're after me."

"They are?"

"Listen, can I come over or what?"

"Of course!"

John Lee lives at home with his parents up in Simi Valley. His parents are awake to greet her, his black mother, his Asian father, both of them so fucking sweet and shiny.

"God Bless you, dear," says his mom, handing Madeline a cup of tea and a plate of amazing cookies that Madeline gobbles up selfishly without remorse.

"How are you holding up after the death of your friend?" his father asks.

"Meh," says Madeline.

"Well, take comfort in the fact that he is happy now, with God, and with Jesus."

How can these people be so shiny and sweet, even at two in the morning? They are too nice, and she is too tired to tell them straight how everything they believe is a bunch of bullshit, even if she *was* down on her luck enough to accept Jesus into her heart.

"Ah, thanks," she says. "I'll try."

And then they all sit down at the kitchen table like it's share time.

"Well, I'm pretty tired…," Madeline says, trying to segway into bedtime.

"I find," the dad of John Lee says, "that taking comfort in Jesus is the only way to truly make sense of all the pain in this world. So please know, young lady, that your friend is saved."

And Madeline has to choke on her cookie, a little.

"Um — he wasn't saved, he is totally fucking dead and

his ashes right now are being spread who knows where in Germany, a country which certainly doesn't fucking need any more people in the form of ashes."

She didn't mean to swear in front of them, but she can't fucking help it. She is fucking pissed. Even if they are fucking saving her from the fucking Vampires right now, the presumption that they think they can save someone from death is just too much to fucking bear.

John Lee's mom touches her hand. As if she's read her mind.

"Saved doesn't mean being saved from death," John Lee's mom says. "Salvation means being saved from a life of meaninglessness. Salvation means your suffering meant something, that your soul can find its home in the light instead of the darkness."

Where his mom stops, his dad picks up.

"Yes! And He saves us from our human conception of JUSTICE."

"Well…," Madeline swallows. They are protecting her from the Vampires tonight, be polite, she insists in her head, just nod and then everyone will go to bed, go to bed, Christ, she just wants some fucking sleep.

And then Madeline realizes where John Lee got his God-talk-a-lot. If John is Prince-preach-a-lot, his dad is King–preach-a-lot, and don't even try and stop him at two o'clock in the morning.

"God! God is all, and the Almighty is the movement that made the universe from matter the size of a marble. God! God is near and far and everywhere and nowhere. God is the storm, raging, and God is the eye of the storm, calm. God is right and righteous, perfect and unassailable." And then John Lee's dad drops his voice like a thrilling secret. "But Jesus is love, a perfect love — a love that is unconditional and for all of us. A sacred heart in which we are all held."

His voice a song now, in a minor key.

"Jesus weeps. Because he knows our joy, and our pain, and our sorrow. But his sorrow is greater than all of ours. Not because of his death, but because of a sadness that comes from loving humans, and having his sacred heart broken, again and again."

He takes his wife's hand.

"We are thankful you have come to us for help," he finishes in a different voice. "Sleep well."

And they both hug her goodnight, for Christ's sake.

Madeline doesn't want to talk to John Lee, who is staring at her, not leaving his own living room. She wants to sleep on the little couch they set up for her that looks like a dream — like a fucking dream — right now.

"So… I'm really tired," she says again.

"The Vampires are really after you?" Lee asks, gently.

"Well, I am poking the nest, so to speak. I am telling them I have evidence against them, implicating them in his death."

He looks at her with a "*quoi?*" expression.

"I know they killed him," she says, "and they tried to make it look like a suicide."

"How do you know that?"

"He was scared. They threatened him, and the cross — that cross you gave me — I gave it to him. And it wasn't there. That cross was gone. They took it off him. That's how I know they did it. And now that they know that I know, and that I am going to have revenge on them, they are going to come after *me*."

"Revenge?"

"I am gonna stake Vince Vaughn."

John Lee blinks. "I don't think that is a good idea, Madeline."

She shrugs.

"What Would Jesus Do?" he asks.

"I don't care what he'd do. He had his chance and did what he did. What am *I* gonna do, that's the question."

Chapter 29:
Gray Hardware

When Dominique Colt pleaded for her life in front of a jury of her peers, it was all anyone could do to not throw up, guffaw, or congratulate her on a great performance. But those reactions would all be in contempt of court.

The collective jury sitting in their living rooms had the luxury to do all three. And mourn. It was the stirring conclusion of what had been months of great television. It had everything that made for a great spectacle: An evil and attractive accused, brutal sexuality, horrific murder, cult-religion, quack-psychology... and of course, a mystery man.

The Mystery Man.

Madeline sighs. As if there were such a thing in the modern world.

The Vampires tracked her easily, of course. Dieter had given them all of her information. So when the number she didn't recognize called and a guy said he was Vince Vaughn's agent and he heard she had a script for Vince… she decided she better hit the hardware store and acquire a proper weapon.

Unfortunately, they don't make stakes like the ones she needs.

She finds herself walking through the aisles of Al's Hardware, listening to the Muzak. Looking at the gray concrete floor. Gray, gray, gray. Everything here feels fifty shades of gray. The colors not the book. Looking around at the ladders and chains and thinking of what a stupid book that is. Don't they meet at a hardware store or something? What a ridiculous place to have anyone accidentally run into anyone.

She needs to focus. Back to reality:

What is the best way to kill a modern Vampire in the form of Vince Vaughn?

Madeline touches a piece of wood. She looks up at the older man, gray hair coming from his ears. He walks aimlessly, needing direction. Yes — she should give that to him, being a director and all — but she is too busy having her moment.

Her hand caresses the wood. It could be anything:

A stake.

A cross.

It is neither and both right now. Neither exist.

Nor does this:

A red contact floating on the cheek of her dead friend. For now, it is just something in her mind. That time is gone.

The only thing she has is right now.

Chapter 30: Delivery Boy

She is meeting him at his agent's office. An anorexic woman with gigantic breasts squeezed into a business attire top leads her into a back room. Madeline is chewing piece after piece of gum. She realizes that she, who never lets them see her sweat (or cry), is nervous. She is fucking nervous to meet Vince Vaughn. Even if she thinks he is a shitty actor who does shitty movies.

She is told to wait, and he'll be right with her.

And the door closes. But she can see into the dark shadows, he is already there. Vampire Vince Vaughn, his eyes bright, but not red unless it's just from being hung-over.

"Hey there, baby," he says.

"Who you calling, 'baby'?" Mads says.

"It's a joke," says Vince. "I call every girl, 'baby,'"

"I'm not a girl, I'm a woman, so don't call me 'baby,' Vince Vaughn."

"No need to get touchy. What are you, some feminist or something? You're the one who wanted this meeting."

"Right. I know."

Vince Vaughn gets closer. "I just wanna know, baby, if you're a Juice Box, a spy, or a legitimate director."

"Maybe I'm all three," Madeline says.

"Well, let's suck it and see," he says, and he moves in.

Madeline doesn't even need much force — she just puts her fist up and he runs his face into it. Blood is squirting from his nose in a very satisfying way.

Vince Vaughn screams and slaps her across the cheek.

She knees him hard in his balls and pulls out the piece of wood.

It is a giant cross. The end is sharpened to a point good enough to stab him through the heart.

He starts to laugh. "Seriously, baby?"

"Seriously, baby."

"I could beat the shit out of you in two seconds. But to tell you the truth I'm kinda turned on right now. Not because you're hot, but because that punch just really woke me up."

"And I think I would like to put a stake through your heart, and fucking kill you for killing my friend."

Vince takes out a smoke, his nose is bleeding like crazy.

"Look," he says, "I don't know what evidence you think you have, but I'm here to tell you this — your friend did himself in. I told him he was out of The Order and that ruined his fucking life."

"Ha!" she says. It's all she can muster.

Vince shrugs. "But yeah, a suicide associated with The Order doesn't look good, so we'd love to keep it from going any further."

She holds her cross/stake out in her best fencing move. "I'm gonna stake you through the heart, Vince Vaughn," she says, smirking.

Does he look scared? Maybe. It is hard to read emotion on that puss of his. "I think you'd rather cast me in your movie," he says. "Because I think we could really help each other."

He lit the smoke. It's illegal to smoke indoors in California, but he's Vince Vaughn. The Vampire. He doesn't give a fuck. He does that thing with his eyes that he did in "Swingers." He likes her, now. She has him. She could stake him without too much trouble, and she knows it.

But he could be a real asset to her movie — that is for sure.

She stalls. "Do you happen to know George Clooney?" she asks.

"*Know* him," Vince says with a grin. "I fuck him every night and twice before breakfast."

Madeline lowers her stake and steals one of his smokes. "Oh, fuck you," she says.

And then he lights the cigarette for her. "Listen, baby," he says. "You and I both know you're bluffing."

"Oh, I know I'm bluffing," she says. "You don't."

"You just told me," he says.

"That's part of my genius," Mads says. "I tell you I'm bluffing so you think I'm bluffing not knowing how I am going to fuck your career from here to Thursday with this Vampire shit. When it gets out that you're a Vampire — and a murderer."

"Listen, baby — Madeline, I mean, Madeline-baby, Baby Mads," he says, blowing smoke out of his bloody nose. "I like you. I do. I really like you. And so, I'd rather we be professional about this. You shut the fuck up, and I'll do your little movie for the SAG Low-Budget rate plus back-end. That's the deal."

Vince Vaughn would be a real feather in the cap. Vince Vaughn as Felix. Vince Vaughn as the one who gets his throat slit — would there be some vicarious justice in that?

Her going to jail for killing Vince Vaughn isn't going to bring Dieter back.

And in the end, after all, isn't she, Madeline Hunter, a completely selfish cunt who only cares for her own career?

She could give Dieter an 'in memoriam' at the end of the movie, before the credits roll.

"Don't you, like, improvise all the time?" she asks, inhaling.

"Yeah, never the same take twice," Vince Vaughn says.

"I hate that," Madeline says. "I fucking hate that improv shit."

"Take it or leave it, baby," Vince says.

Chapter 31: The Mystery of the Cross

So it's okay to go home, she guesses. To pick up the mail, see if her cactus is still alive. It's the middle of the day, and she and Vince have come to an understanding, she supposes. She has a clean stake under her arm, a few of his cigarettes in her purse and his blood beneath her nails. He is going to be a real ass on set, and she knows it.

There is a stack of mail at her front door.

Bills, bills, junk mail, a letter from her dead friend.

Extreme Close-Up: Letter from Dieter, post-marked the day he died.

She knows what it must be. A confession. A suicide note. Something the Vampires made him write to get people off their trail. They forged it or forced him to write it, killed him and dropped it in the mail. She can see it now. They'd claim he wrote it and then walked that night to that mail drop down the street, before OD'ing on a crap cocktail of Vampire-transforming drugs.

She regrets not staking Vince Vaughn. Oh but, she'll get another chance. First she'll expose them all for being the blood-letting fuckheads they are —

— It looks like he'd taken his time with her name though. He used the block letters he sometimes favored, and even the little cartoon golem-girl he drew of her next to her name:

𝕸𝖆𝖉𝕾 𝕳𝖚𝖓𝖙𝖊𝖗

Her address was written in the fairy-tale calligraphy he busted out when he really cared.

Of the Studio City

Her hands are shaking, and she has to light a cigarette and take a deep drag before deciding whether to open it or take it straight to the police. There is something besides paper inside the envelope — on a small chain — and she can feel its shape.

"No," she says, tearing it open, accidentally ripping the cartoon drawing of her right across the head.

If he'd written it under duress, he'd taken his sweet time in that duress. Each letter was prettily formed:

"I am sorry" is all it said.

And there is the missing cross.

Alone, like blood coming from every pore, she cries.

Jesus wept.

Chapter 32:
A Perfect Day
for Banana Peels

It's dark in Casa Vega, but it is always dark in Casa Vega. Mads sees someone at the bar. It's him again. She quickly averts her gaze, but she can't help seeing that he looks terrible. Maybe it's because he doesn't have his three-piece suit on. Hopefully he doesn't see her, but no dice. And she can't seem to get out of the fact that he is now coming over to her and sitting at her table.

How does one talk to such a person?

"Uh, hi, Mr. Snow," she says.

"Madeline Hunter! How are you?"

She says what she is expected to say. "I'm doing well. You?"

The fact that it is the middle of the school day and he is

in ill-fitting shorts with weepy-looking eyes belie his reply of, "Oh, I'm fine."

"Isn't it a school day?" she asks.

"Oh, I lost that job at Well-Spring some years back. Laid off."

Shit.

"Oh, well," she says, doing her best attempt to make him feel better. "Honestly, there's no shittier job than being a teacher, right? Even flipping burgers, you probably get more respect."

"Yeah, it's better," he agrees with her, and finishes his drink. "For awhile it was worse, but then it got better. I met a lady — I went through some weird times and well, the wife left, the kid hates me — I don't have a job, but hey, at least I'm happy, right?"

"That's great!" she says, her face horrified.

"Damn Skippy!" he says, "I'm fucking thrilled!"

Jesus. He is. He looks like shit, but there is a maniacal glint in his eye that she recognizes now — it is the glint of someone with nothing to lose who is therefore actually L to the I to the V to the I to the N. They're the most dangerous cats out there. The livin' ones.

"Oh, yeah," he continues. "I'm following my dreams now. I never wanted to be a teacher. I always wanted to be a comedian, and now, I'm really working toward that."

Jesus, she wants to crawl in a hole and die for him, just about now.

He has been taking classes at the Manic People Party, a long-form improvisation troupe where all the new famous people are being culled from. They have a twenty-two tier organizational structure of classes. He is at tier two. So he is learning how to be an improviser. He has a flyer for his next show, and he invites her to see it.

The idea of poor Mr. Snow, once a proud man, improvising in some small theater, working his way up through the levels of some pyramid-scheme improv society... oh well. Whatever.

"Of course I'll come!" she says, looking at the flyer.

God, please let him leave now... she thinks. "Definitely!" she says, to provoke him to leave.

But he is still sitting there, with his strange half-smile expression. Boy, she never really did appreciate how much of a sad-sack comedian face he had.

"We do this game," he says, "that really, to me, is the key to life."

"Hm?" she says, not wanting to give him too much.

"It's called, 'Acceptance.' It's based on the concept of 'Yes, and…'"

"Hm?"

"Oh, you missed an easy one there Madeline. You should say, 'Yes, and…?'"

No, but then you would keep talking, she thinks to herself, but too many years of being his pupil have made her dutiful, chagrined, forced into submission. "Sorry," she says, instead.

He accepts her apology with grace and chirpily explains:

"This game is from a type called the Chester. In this game, we start with a relationship and a one-word phrase. From this you build the scene. The only rule is that you must accept what your partner says or does. 'YES, AND…,' that is your mantra. If the phrase is 'The baby is eating too many bananafish again,' you might choose to slip on the peel. I felt foolish the first time I tried it, but I soon found that slipping on bananafish peels is something I am really good at. I feel alive. It is scary, how alive I feel."

"Hm," she says. "I mean. 'Yes, and…?'"

He laughs. "Good! And what are you doing drinking here in the middle of the afternoon, young lady?"

"I'm waiting for my Mystery Man," she says.

"Yes, and…?" he says with a laugh. "Here I am!"

And just like that, everything stops.

The apocalypse happens.

She was blind, but now she sees, and the first shall be the last and the last the first.

The Passion and The Mystery — enacted in real murdered boy-blood, immaculately conceived in her mind as George Clooney — space-time fuck at Casa Vega in this moment. Manifest destiny is here in the form of her former math teacher. He is shining with a halo of revelation before her. She knows now who he really is, really.

"Yes, and…," she can finally mutter.

Then he puts his fingers to his lips, turns them like a key.

He stands up. She is still seated, but he bends over and hugs her.

She can smell his sweat, his animal nature. If she raised her head to his, he'd kiss her lips, she knows it. She can't feel whether she would like this or it would make her throw up a little in her mouth. She certainly does not raise her head to him, though. But she can feel his heart beating in his chest. And it is a sacred heart. She feels its beat and knows it is true.

A sacred heart.

"Please come see my show," he says as a parting. And he staggers off.

She stares after him, watching him go to the door. She hopes he isn't driving.

She stares into the space he left for some time.

"Fuck," she says aloud. Then she says it again with a long exhale with the weight of the world of words on her shoulder.

"I have to fucking re-write everything."

Epilogue: Pushing Back

BUZZ!

Someone is ringing from the front gate. Dominique walks to the intercom in her apartment, and presses down on the TALK button.

"Hello?" she says, her voice, soft and small.

"Listen, I am very sorry to have not called first but could I please come up?" He sounds like he has been crying.

"Oh… uh… it's not a good time," she says, noticing that she has got some head stuffing on the intercom.

"Please, please. I beg of you. My life depends on it."

Ironic?

Life and Death. Life or Death. Now for him, too. She buzzes him in. She goes to the sink to wash her hands.

Now, what was the plan?

She was writing 'Nosferatu' on the wall in blood — that's right.

It is a bit like a lucid dream, a part of her understanding that she is in shock right now and the simplicity and normalcy of washing her hands or having a visitor is helping her from dissolving into high-pitched screams.

There is the knock.

She opens the door, only slightly, to see Mr. Snow. He has definitely been crying.

"Listen," he starts and talks a long stream that ends with, " — I need you to help me or I swear to God… or I swear to nothingness… I cannot live another day."

Dominique opens the door wide and tells him to come in.

He walks past her, then seeing something so grotesque and unbelievable he is certain it is a practical joke. She closes the door and leans up against it.

"Uh…," he says.

Dominique thinks she should probably pick up the brick and bash in Mr. Snow, too, after all. What's a third after she'd already done two, and he was actually suicidal, so maybe it would be doing him a favor. But at that moment she can't really muster much energy for anything, so she stands leaning against his only exit.

"Now, what has happened here?" Snow asks in his most reasonable tone.

"I slit his throat, stabbed him and beat him to death with a brick," she says, motioning toward the left. "And then I did the same to that one," she says, pointing toward the right.

"Oh, and why did you do that?" he asks, as if he was asking a student to answer why they used that particular method of factoring to find the root of a polynomial.

She shrugs. "I just felt like I had to," she says. She brings a hand to her head. She has washed that hand, but not well enough that it didn't leave a red mark on her that reminds him of Ash Wednesday.

"Well," he says. "That's…very…," and then he vomits.

She doesn't move to assist him.

"So," she says, "I've got a lot to do in here, but if you want to go in the other room we can do a session."

He wipes off his mouth with his sleeve.

There is HOLYFUCKINGSHIT DEATH EVERY-WHERE, and in her eyes, horror and madness. And he realizes he has never, nope not ever, truly been scared like this before. Still, he can get out of here with his life, he knows it. She isn't holding a weapon, he outweighs her by at least 70 pounds, he is a head and a half taller than her, and at that exact moment she seems so stunned she probably would just step aside and let him out.

But his wife is leaving him, and doesn't love him, and he has wasted every moment of his pathetic life, and she is the only thing that has kept him going, so here he is. This is it. He will live or die now, and it is entirely up to her. That was what he had wanted — that was what he had asked for — to put his life in her hands. Of course, he hadn't realized she was psychotically murderous when he said that, but that was the risk you took when you willingly placed your life in someone else's hands.

"So do you want that session, now?" she asks

And so, Bert Snow, age 46, chronically depressed, suicidal, and on the brink of divorce, decides to go ahead with his reason for coming in the first place.

There is a universe filled with answers to his question, but he asks it anyway.

"Why not?"

She walks him into the other room.

She turns on the light.

The room is clean, like the last time he had been in there. But there is no chair or chain.

"Oh," she says, realizing, "I just used both of them on — "

And she stops short of saying their names, but she gestures generally in the direction of the other room.

"I'll go get them," she says.

And she leaves the room.

He hears the unhooking of the chain, the fall of the body as it slumps to the floor. She wheels the chair and chain in, both covered with blood and who knows what else.

"I should clean them," she says, vaguely, but then makes no move to do so.

She hits the timer.

"So," she says, "tell me what's going on."

She smells so much of blood, of her own sweat, and she, hands shaking and leaving red trails wherever they go, unbuttons his shirt.

"I… uh… my wife is leaving me," he stammers. "And I, uh, she says she hasn't, uh, been happy for a while, which is, uh, hardly surprising, but I guess I uh uh uh…" and she has his shirt off, and her hands with blood caked under the fingernails, but her hands are actually clean, and then he realizes it's her sleeves that are still soaked with blood. "I guess I was surprised, though. I guess I was really surprised."

"So you came here for therapy."

"I actually almost threw myself off the 5 overpass onto oncoming traffic, because I was like fuck L.A., and fuck traffic, and fuck this life. But…"

She is unbuttoning his pants now.

"But then I thought about our last therapy session, and I realized how much that had helped and — "

"Oh, do you know that I actually bought ice cream, just in case that's what you requested — remember how you wanted a milkshake?"

"Yes."

He is surprised that he is fully erect, and that in fact, two dead men lay less than fifteen feet past him, and knowing he would very likely be next acted as an aphrodisiac, and he is having a very difficult time keeping his hands off her as had been their agreement, and while he didn't know what had happened with the two before him, he didn't think this was the best time to test the boundaries.

"Have a seat," she says.

Now, putting his naked flesh on the seat with blood and piss and whatever else —

She turns with a direct look.

He sits quickly.

She drags the chain over and wraps him in it. She locks the padlock and puts the blindfold over his eyes.

Before she puts the gag in, she says, "Bert, today, as a final session of your radical therapy, I can grant your wish. I must warn you, you will probably suffer greatly before it ends, because I do not seem to be very good at quick and painless death. I may just have to kill you regardless, but, well, I'm open to your opinion on the matter."

The timer hasn't dinged yet, but she leaves and shuts the door, anyway.

So he is in there now, blinded, and knowing this is it. He is going to most likely die now, and in a completely unanticipated way. He thinks of his wife finding out, her shock. He now finds it exciting, that she will find out and think he was having a kinky affair. He thinks of his son and how mortified Parker will be and how fucked up for life he will be. Oh well. At least his son will have no illusions. That's better, isn't it?

He thinks of the feeling of the fluid from the dead boys in the other room on his naked ass. He thinks about how now that he has thrown up, he is hungry. He is still erect, and he thinks how much he would like, before he dies, to gently make love with his killer.

He thinks about what a funny situation this is.

He thinks, if he lives, he will go back to comedy. Fuck teaching.

And he hears her in the other room, moving things around and talking to herself, saying things he could almost make out like:

"Fuck you, this is your fault, Felix!" — and her making the sound of physical exertion — she is stabbing his dead body again and again for good measure.

And then he hears a DING.

And hears her coming back to him. And he starts shaking.

Actually, he thinks he *does* want to live. He does. He actually does.

He hears her open the door.

"What would you like to drink?" her voice asks calmly.

"I'll have a milkshake now," he says.

"Chocolate or vanilla?"

A dying man's last thing to drink. A milkshake. Chocolate or vanilla? He really didn't know that could be such an important question. Typically, he would just say chocolate, but there is something about the simplicity of the flavor of vanilla, something that would remind him of childhood and soft-serve.

"Vanilla," he says. "Please."

And she leaves again.

He can hear the blender going in the other room. She comes back with a glass full of white cream. The milkshake is the most delicious thing he has ever tasted in his whole life, ever. He tells her.

"This is the best milkshake I've ever had in my life."

"Really? I tried to get good ice cream, and you know, organic milk."

"It's amazing, It's the most incredibly amazing milkshake ever."

"Thank you!"

"What are you doing out there?"

"Oh, I'm trying to frame the Vampires," she says. "I… well, I had this whole plan. Oh Bert, can I just talk for a second? I know this is *your* therapy, but if it's okay, I'd really like to talk about *me* for a minute. Can I?"

"Of course!" he says. "Do you want to take off my blindfold so you can see me look sympathetically into your eyes?"

"No, that's okay," she says. "That will make it more difficult if I have to beat you to death with a brick. Honestly, I feel positively haunted already by both Felix and Jim's eyes and I wish I'd blinded them or something, just blinded them so they couldn't look at me."

In order to deter her from getting more excited about blinding him he says, "So, you wanted to discuss…"

"Oh, I just, I really… I just really did something really really terrible — I'm sure you saw the results."

As if it were possible he hadn't.

"Yes," he says.

"I was just kind of thinking how strange it is that you didn't run away screaming."

"I'm *that* depressed," he says.

It is true.

"I guess I *should* kill you," she says. "Oh, but you need your quote."

She lifts his blindfold. He can see into her eyes — pupils dilated like an animal, sex and death and right now at this moment she is deciding whether she will kill him or let him go.

"The quote?" he reminds her, gently.

She has never really understood what it meant when people said that their heart might "burst," but she feels it in that moment. Her chest feels constricted, she is in danger of crying, and that wouldn't do. So she sits on his lap in the chair, and feels his naked humanity enveloping her, and the smell of sweat and whatever special pheromonal concoction puberty decided would be his human cologne.

He holds her in his arms and she shudders, not crying.

She says, "This is from Camus:

'In the midst of winter, I found there was, within me, an invincible summer.'" Her voice becomes a low tremor. She is telling him something now, she is revealing to him, now, the secret of his universe. He has to be quiet, very quiet.

"*'And that makes me happy. For no matter how hard the world pushes against me, within me, there's something stronger, something better, pushing right back.'*

'Pushing right back.'"

And then she parts her legs, straddles him on the chair, and slides his cock inside her.

"Life or death," she says. "Which will it be?"

And as they make love, he looks into the eyes of his death.

Does he know, which? Which he chooses?

She does. As he climaxes, she sees his choice in perfect clarity.

She lifts herself off of him. She kisses his lips.

"Go," she says.

But she is the one who leaves, who walks out of the room, then right out the front door, leaving it open.

He stands up. He is no longer shaking.

He puts his clothes on.

He doesn't look at the room he must walk through — a room of death, death of those younger than him, brighter than him, better loved than him — he must not see it, he must focus on just one thing. Just one thing now. He focuses his eyes only on the open door that he is going to walk through. Right now.

Each step his will to live.

Each step a Yes, and…

I will live.

I will live.

I will.

ACKNOWLEDGMENTS

Gratitude to John Skipp, Ezra Werb, Carolynne Dale Levine, Francesca Lia Block, Rose O'Keefe, Jim Agpalza, Matthew Revert, Cameron Pierce, my Bizarro tribe, and you.

ABOUT THE AUTHOR

Laura Lee Bahr is the author of the Wonderland Book Award winning novel, *Haunt*, which has been translated into Spanish by Orciny Press (*Fantasma*). Her short stories appear in various anthologies. She is an independent filmmaker, actor, and whatever else she needs to do to cry out the sacred profanity of this human experience. She lives in Los Angeles with her long-time sweetheart and feline family.

INDIEGOGO CAMPAIGN HALL OF FAME THANKS!!!

Michael Arnzen * David S. Atkinson * David Bridges * Natalie Briggs * John Bruni * Bob Brustman * Brian Bubonic * Hugo Camacho * Maraluce Catherine * RJ Cavender * Chad * Colleen The Tax Queen Cassidy * Mike Christian * John Wayne Comunale * N.C. Christopher Couch * Kyle Dare * Jarrid Deaton * Etienne Deforest * Hollie DeFrancisco * Robert Devereaux * Mr. T Duke * Frank Edler * Scott Eubanks * Karl Fischer * Dan Fisk * Constance Ann Fitzgerald * Rebecca "Soup" Franich * Rodney Gardner * His Majesty Eirik Gumeny, Lord of the Fly Girls * James Henry Hall * Jane Hamilton * Brad C. Hodson * Steven M Irwin * Jeremy Robert Johnson * Shawn Jones * Andrew Kasch * Ed Kemper * Jan Kozlowski * James Frederick Leach * Sean Leonard * Chin Li * Michael Ling * Kevin Lintner * Jonathan Maberry * Anton Major * Josh Spicoli Martens * Tracie McBride * Brian McClain * Nick Mozak * Charles Austin Muir * Sauda Namir * CS Nelson * Aaron Nemoyten * Michael Noe * Kit O'Connell * Marnie Olson * J David Osborne * Nicholaus Patnaude * Charles Pinion * Teresa Pollack * Scott Rabin * Martin Roberts * Michael Allen Rose * ryanrockshard * Tiffany Scandal * Tanya Semmons * Eric Siegel * Greg Sisco * Bix Skahill * Rick Slater * Virginia Slater * Curt Sobolewski * Kevin Strange * Deana Uutela * Kerry Vail * Matthew Vaughn * Marvin P Vernon * Grant M. Wamack Jr. * Tabitha Warrick * Ian Welke * Rick Westbrock * Frances Winkler * Mandy Zeller

www.ingramcontent.com/pod-product-compliance
Lightning Source LLC
Chambersburg PA
CBHW070115030726
47506CB00002B/748